About the Author

Francis Lord lives and works in Manchester. This is his first
novel.

Jade
The Scarred Journey

Francis Lord

Jade
The Scarred Journey

Olympia Publishers
London

www.olympiapublishers.com
OLYMPIA PAPERBACK EDITION

A CIP catalogue record for this title is
available from the British Library.

ISBN: 978-1-80439-796-1

This is a work of fiction.
Names, characters, places and incidents originate from the writer's
imagination. Any resemblance to actual persons, living or dead, is
purely coincidental.

First Published in 2024

Olympia Publishers
Tallis House
2 Tallis Street
London
EC4Y 0AB

Printed in Great Britain

Dedication

For my mum and Nicholas.

Prologue

It was the night everything changed. But Jade Hall didn't know it yet.

After all, she was only a baby. Wrapped in small blankets placed on her parents' bed in their city centre flat on Whitworth Street.

The police found her in the wardrobe. Hidden away and covered over with several sheets.

Jade was beginning to cry. Surrounded by people she did not know in uniforms she had not seen before. This was not a comfortable atmosphere for the young baby. She was picking up the tense and serious vibes from the many strangers who were now in her parents' flat.

It was time to go.

An officer gently picked up Jade. Carrying her out of the flat. To do so, the officer would need to take her through the flat corridor towards the main door.

But the gunfire had made the door become totally destroyed. The door was collapsed now on the floor of the corridor.

The officer saw further down the flat towards the study.

The officers in the study looked down at the two dead corpses of Jade's parents. Bullet shots through both their heads. The carpet soaked up in their blood. These officers were standing in the heart of the crime scene. Taking photos and camera recordings.

There was nothing left to see here. The officer took Jade out of the flat. A place that was home for Jade. Never to be her home ever again.

The police never did find who murdered Jade's parents. In this city, it was harder than ever for them to solve crimes. Keeping the peace was the goal they aimed for.

And the murders have now changed everything.

From now on, Jade would know everything would be different. Setting Jade on a new journey that had now been forced upon her.

Chapter 1

The echoed screams stayed with Jade deep within her subconscious. Appearing again and again in her dreams. The screams. The bullet shots. Year after year.

Jade had to wake up. She was tossing and turning on her bed. But she could not wake up. The dream would not let her. Then, the sound of the bullet was so loud in her dream that it woke her up instantly, like the sound of an alarm clock.

Her eyes shot open instantly. She caught her breath to get her bearings. Looking up, she saw a familiar face of a white-haired woman in her early fifties sat on the edge of Jade's bed, looking down at her.

Still not fully awake, Jade tried to remember where she was. She sat up from her bed. The tossing and turning in her sleep made her long black hair cover over her face. Sweeping her hair aside, she looked around to see herself in a small room with two beds, a sink, a table, and metal bars covering the windows.

Of course, I'm still in Alpha City Prison. My home, Jade thought.

Her breathing began to slow down as she became more conscious. Sitting up, she looked over to her white-haired cellmate called Eve. Eve had a calm warmth to her personality that Jade appreciated. A warmth almost maternal. Something Jade knew little about. To help relax Jade, Eve placed her hand gently on Jade's shoulder.

'Bad dreams again?' Eve asked.

'Voices, sounds. Nightmares,' Jade replied.

Eve looked concerned for her young friend Jade. She knew there was a deep scar troubling her within her heart. And she knew there was more than one scar buried deep within her.

*

Sometime later, the female prison mates were together being served their evening meal in the prison canteen. With several queuing for food and others already sat eating their meals. Some talking to their cellmate friends, or others watching the T.V. It was placed on a high shelf near the top corner of the canteen.

On TV, a news reporter gave the latest news on the city headlines.

Good evening. In today's news, police across the city have been put on standby following reports of riots and fighting within businessman Jack Kane's Alpha Central territory. Since the treaty was signed to appease the powerful business gang lord Jack Kane, a treaty that gave himself security and business control of Alpha Central several years ago, crime has risen sixty per cent across the city. With fear the crimes could grow throughout the city, newly elected Alpha City Mayor Paul Gordon is working closely with police to ensure the safety of the people of Alpha City.

*

Elsewhere in the prison, Jade stayed busy at work in a specially built gym. Aiming to stay fit and healthy. Doing sit-ups, press-ups, bench presses, etc. Spending time hitting hard at a boxing punch bag with both her feet and fisted hands. Similar in style to Ultimate Fighting athletes. Also, spending time on a rowing machine. Training alone. The way she likes it.

After training, Jade took a long, hot shower. A young woman in her early twenties, Jade looked slim and athletic, with a slight muscular figure. Her long, black, wet hair fell down to under her chest. She was a woman who had balanced out the need to be fit and athletic yet remained very feminine and beautiful.

Finishing her shower, she dried herself off alone in the shower area. Placing on her prison shirt and pants that were placed on a nearby table and bench. Suddenly, she heard the door to the shower area open up. Jade had her back to the door. She waited to hear the sounds of footsteps on the tile floor. She could hear them overlapping each other.

There must be two or three of them in the room, Jade thought. *No echoes; I think there are three.* Jade did not let them stop her. She continued to dress and put on her clothes. Now fully clothed, the group of women now stood right behind Jade.

'Jade Hall,' said one of the female group with a Scottish accent. *I recognise that voice,* Jade thought.

She turned around to face the group of female prisoners. Jade looked directly at the Scottish female. She recognised her, but she looked different to what she remembered. The Scottish woman was slim and well-built, with a short back and sides brown hair.

'Sam Stewart?' Jade said. 'Am I right? You murdered the wife and kids of the guy you were sleeping with. I remember you. You had a sharp eye for being a sniper with a gun.'

'Good memory,' replied Sam.

'You were one of my early cases. You're thinner than I remember you.'

'I've had practice to build up muscle with my fists. Against a lot of other women in this place. Never thought I'd see you in here with the rest of us. We're now the same, Jade. Equals.'

'If that's the case, are you wanting to prove a point, Sam? If you are, I'm ready. Tell your friends to back off.'

Sam turned her head to the left and right. Directing the other two women to step back and give Jade and Sam space. Looking back at the other, both stared deep into the other person's eyes. Both not even daring to blink.

'You first,' Jade offered.

Sam walked up to Jade and punched her really hard in the face. The force of the punch pushed Jade back several paces. When she stopped, she stood still for a few seconds. Mentally, she focused on her body. Composing her strength. Then she moved to stand back up straight, looking strong. Then she stared back into the eyes of Sam.

'Now it's my turn bitch,' spoke Jade.

Jade started running towards Sam. Grabbing her, pushing, and forcing Sam up against the wall. Jade started punching Sam hard again and again in the ribs and stomach before moving up the body towards the face.

But Sam started hitting back several times at Jade's face. The hits made Jade step back away from Sam but took her chance. Pushing and forcing Jade back into one of the shower cubicles. Sam slammed Jade's body up against the shower cubicle wall. Switching on the shower tap. The water poured down over Jade's body, distracting her. Sam punched, hitting hard at Jade's body. Being strong and relentless. Making sure each hit her with force. With each punch, Sam remembered back to how Jade had pursued her all over the city. Then, capturing her. Having her locked up in this place. She was enjoying this beating as revenge.

14

But still, at the back of her mind, she thought, what had Jade done to be locked up in here?

Jade was now looking worn down and beaten. Sam grabbed her soaking-wet shirt and dragged Jade out of the cubicle. Throwing her towards the nearby table and bench. Sam threw her on top of the table. Jade rolled across it. Falling and crashing down on the tile floor on the other side.

Sam looked at the other two women standing a good distance away. She looked pleased with herself, feeling she had won this fight.

'You see, Jade, you have to know your place and where you stand in a prison like this.'

On the floor, Jade opened her eyes as Sam spoke. All wet, Jade had cuts on her face. Blood started to fall down her face from the cuts. Bruises started to form on her rib area. She could feel the pain. All of it. This was the moment she was trained for. She focused her mind and turned inward.

This pain will not hold me down, she thought. *This pain will not hold me back. This pain is a wall.*

I must break through and fight back. Stand up, Jade. Get up. The pain is your challenge to overcome. Your strength is more powerful than the pain. Never let anyone hold you down. Now get up. Get up. Now.

Jade picked herself up off the cold floor. Anger now started to fuel her heart. Her eyes fixed and locked on Sam. Sam looked at Jade in amazement. Jade stood up once again, ready for Sam. Sam stood poised, ready to dish out more punishment.

Sam ran up to Jade. Her fist was ready to hit Jade right in the face. Even harder this time. Then, Jade grabbed with her hand Sam's clenched fist. Holding it back. The force and power from Jade to hold the fist back shocked Sam and Sam tried hard to force her fist forward. Jade's hold was far stronger. She stared deep and calm into the eyes of Sam. Jade's eyes now looked sharper and more focused, looking into the fearful growing eyes of Sam.

'You've now lost,' Jade whispered quietly.

She turned her hand that held Sam's clenched fist upward and then moved it back towards Sam's face. The odd angle of the arm caused pain in Sam's arm, forcing her knees to bend. With every second, Sam looked smaller and smaller next to Jade.

Then, with her free hand, Jade punched Sam real hard in the face. She let go of her grip on Sam's clenched fist. Letting Sam collapse on the floor below. Jade kicked hard and fast into Sam's body and face. The other two females looked on, fearful at Jade. Helpless to stop what was happening. Seeing the fire of rage in Jade's eyes.

Jade picked up the dazed Sam off the floor. Throwing her body down hard on the nearby table. Sam laid on her back with her head and neck, leaning off the edge of the table. Jade walked once around the table. Almost animal-like. Stalking around her fallen prey. She stopped still once, standing by the side of the table where Sam's leaning head and neck were placed. Jade lifted one of her legs above Sam's head. Then, bent her knee, placing her leg around Sam's neck. Starting to press her leg together. Strangling Sam so hard. Sam's face started to turn red, then blue. Struggling for breath, Sam was mere seconds from being killed by Jade.

'Now I'm like you, Sam, what've I got left to lose?' Jade said in anger.

Jade continued pressing her leg tight around Sam's neck. She refused to let go. Sam now struggled desperately to breathe.

'JADE!' Eve screamed out.

Jade turned and looked back at the doorway. Eve was standing there. She walked quickly up towards Jade. As she did, Jade let go of her grip ever so slightly on Sam. But not too much.

'Jade, what you've got left to lose is your conscience and your heart. Let her go,' Eve said calmly. Jade gave no answer. She began to tighten her grip again around Sam's throat.

'Sean,' Eve said. 'Remember who you were to Sean.' Jade's mind then concentrated on that name.

Sean.

I remember, Jade thought, *he was my world, my heart, my soul, my life.* Jade's love for Sean started to calm her down. Making her relax. In her mind's eye, she remembered the first time she ever saw him. Comparing that moment with the present, she knew what she was doing now was wrong.

Jade then fully loosened her grip and placed her leg back on the floor. Eve gave an order to the other two female prisoners, 'Take Sam back to her cell. Now.'

The two females walked up to the table, dragging Sam's half-conscious body off it and left Jade and Eve alone together. The two women looked back at the other.

'Why do you have to stick your nose in when it's not wanted?' Jade asked.

'Because you're a soul that lost something, someone, when you were a baby girl. The guidance of a mother and father taken from you by an unknown killer.'

'How do you know about that?'

'We have many contacts,' replied Eve.

'We?'

'I once worked for a group called Tekker.'

'Never heard of you.'

'You wouldn't have. We tend to remain hidden in the

shadows.'

'You don't look like a shadow to me, Eve.'

'I took a risk. A mistake. And it exposed me. The Tekker group tipped me off to the police. I was expendable to them.'

'Eve, I'd love to stand here all night, but there's an empty cell with a first aid kit waiting for me.' Jade started to leave. Walking past Eve. As she did, Eve grabbed hold of Jade's arm.

'Jade, there was nothing more you could've done. You have to let it go.' Jade knew exactly what Eve was referring to.

'I can't. It's made me who I am,' replied Jade.

'Just like your friend saving you all those years ago made you who you are? What was his name again?'

'Tanner,' Jade replied, 'Frank Tanner.'

Chapter 2

Many years before, Frank Tanner sat behind his desk alone in his office. A private office in a three-floor building at 68 Dale Street. A back street in the northern Quarter near the centre of Alpha Central. The building had been bought by his father several years earlier for the purpose of serving as private detective offices. Now, Frank was running the office alone after his father's death.

The office had an old-fashioned noir feeling to it. Cabinets, shelves, varnished wooden floor, a central desk with another placed by the wall with a computer on it. There were two doors to the office, one facing opposite the large office window and the other door on the side wall to the left of the main door. The adjoining door to the next office alongside Tanner's.

His office desk was placed in front of the main office window. The blinds to the office were half drawn with lamppost lights from the street outside shining through the gaps of the blinds onto Tanner and his desk. The only light in the room came from a small desk lamp on his table. The rest of the room was pitch dark and unlit.

On this night, Tanner was deep in thought. Feeling shattered and crushed from the day's events. He was in his mid-thirties, slim build, dark hair, attractive looks with stubble hair on his face. But his looks could not hold back the heartbreak seen in his red bloodshot eyes. Nor the pain he felt in his heart.

How could've things gotten so bad, so quick? he thought.

He picked up his full glass of alcohol on the table and threw his drink into his mouth and down his throat. Placing the empty glass on the desk next to his bottle, he leaned over and picked up a photo frame that was placed on his desk. Staring deep into it. In the frame was a picture of himself with his wife and son. All three of them looked very happy. Standing outside a countryside mansion on a pleasant sunny day.

Tanner looked at the photo for so long that he had lost track of the time he had spent looking at it. And the more he stared into it, the more pain he felt coming to the surface.

Just then, his office phone was ringing. He placed the frame back on his desk, picked up the phone and answered the call.

'Yes? Frank Tanner's office… Why?… OK, I'm on my way.'

As he put the phone back on the receiver, he stared again at the frame placed on his desk. Staring at the frame, a great sense of guilt came over him.

Shake it off, Frank, he thought to himself. *Get back into your work mode.*

Stepping up fast from his desk, he grabbed his long brown coat off the coat stand. He grabbed his gun out of his pocket to see if it was loaded which it was. Placing it back in his pocket, he quickly put on his coat, left his office, and locked the door.

*

Tanner drove his car through the city centre of Alpha City. Known as Alpha Central. The whole city landscape had a mixture of buildings and high-rise towers. Some were the old gothic, industrialist architectures of the metropolitan past. Other sites have been redeveloped into modern, newly built, clean, polished, glassy buildings being used as offices, hotels, or flats.

Alpha City had one foot still in the past. And another towards the future. Aiming to regenerate itself and the whole city's image. But still, the past was influencing Alpha City's present.

Tanner slowed his car to a stop. He could see up ahead a crowd of people, police officers and cars.

The crowd gathered outside the Alpha City News building near to the Central Library.

Getting out of his car, Tanner approached several officers. Showing them his identification to them, they let him pass. Walking towards some parked police cars, Tanner recognised a particular officer standing next to them. A former friend called Julius Carver.

Julius was head of the city centre police unit. An ambitious man who was once a very close friend of Tanner's. The same age as him, slim, athletic, good-looking. Also having an edge of cockiness to his demeanour and ego. *To get ahead in this world,* Julius thought, *the ego and assurance of himself would get him further.* Now head of the unit, he was on his way.

As Julius stared up at the news building, he caught sight of Tanner walking towards him. It had been a while since Julius last saw him. And what a difference a few months had made.

To Julius, Tanner looked like a shell of his former self. No more happy smiles or positive aura in him. This was now a man cast under a long shadow. Yet Tanner tried to stay composed, focused and professional under the circumstances. Julius respected Frank for that. After all, they were once the best of friends. Brought up close together like brothers. There was still a slim part of Julius that still cared for him. But the changing of time and age from children to adults now brought up the cracks

21

and differences between the two men. Now, being more fractured and distance between the two men, both knew enough still that it was important to have an ally and to work together professionally. And tonight, Julius knew he had stumbled on something that was of great importance to Tanner.

'Better late than never, Frank,' Julius said.

'I think you know why I'd be late.'

'Trouble at home, is there?'

'She's gone,' Tanner replied. 'She took David too. I don't know where.'

'Well, the apple's fallen high from the tree,' Julius said sarcastically.

'Just shut up about it. Why've you brought me out here?'

'We got a tip-off that Farrell was seen going into this building. We think he's got hostages with him.'

Julius pointed towards a nearby entrance that led to an underground car park.

'He was seen entering the car park in a black van. A passer-by recognised his face from the newspapers. So, I knew you'd been after him for a while. So, I gave you a call. And here you are.'

'Why here? Why this building?'

'Well, you know how much of a nutter he is. He saw how the news was covering him. Probably had some crazed issue with the paper. Whatever the case, he's in there now. You've got your chance, Frank. Now's the time to catch Farrell. He's killed seven victims, hasn't he?'

'Eight. He got another one, two nights ago.'

'Well, it looks like he's got several hostages in there with him. But he knows he can't get away.'

'I don't think he wants to,' Tanner said.

'We just need to free the hostages and start negotiating with him.'

'He's impulsive, impatient, and unpredictable, Julius. He won't wait for any deal. And he won't think twice of killing the hostages.'

'Are you sure?' Julius asked.

'Eight victims tells me, I'm sure. Give me five minutes.'

'You could risk the hostage's life if you're up there.'

'Julius, I can't let more people be killed.'

Just then, instant gunshots were firing down on the officers and crowd. The officers ducked for cover behind police vehicles. Julius and Tanner took cover on the other side of a police car. With the gunshots raining down, the loud echo of bullets spread far around the surrounding area. The crowds of people screaming and running. Several shot down and wounded.

Tanner cautiously paid attention to the sound of the gunshots. Hearing them move left and right of him. He was readying to take his chance. Looking over the bonnet of the car to see which window the bullets were coming from.

The gunman was shooting towards the cars left of Tanner. He lifted his head up more to see the gunman, Farrell, shooting from a sixth-floor window. Tanner got out his gun, keeping his eyes on Farrell's window.

Meanwhile, Julius continued shouting out commands to his nearby officers. 'Get ready to storm the building on my command.'

But Tanner did not hear the command. He had made up his mind and was taking his chance.

Jumping up from behind the police car, he rushed towards the building entrance. Julius caught sight of Tanner, but it was too late to stop him.

23

Full of frustration, Julius ordered a new command to the officers to help give Tanner cover to reach the entrance.

'Aim your fire at the window he shot from. Now!'

All the officers started shooting ferociously at the open office window. Quickly, Farrell ducked for cover. Enough time for Julius to see Tanner enter the building and run towards the staircase and lifts.

*

Now inside the building, Tanner slowed himself down from running and approached the lifts.

Looking at the small screen above each lift, he saw them both being on the sixth floor.

It's too risky to call one, thought Tanner. Farrell could notice the call and would be ready for him.

With that logic, Tanner cautiously, with a gun in hand, made his way up the stairs.

Making his way up, he could hear the echo of gunfire from the floor up above. His eyes looking up the staircase above him. Trying to keep his breathing calm, slow and relaxed.

Upon reaching the closed sixth-floor office door, Tanner gently placed his free hand on the door handle. Slowly turning it, he peered his eye through the small gap in the door he had made. Trying to locate quickly where Farrell was within. On seeing him at the very far end, he opened the door wide enough to step into the large office. Hiding behind a nearby office desk.

The office floor was made up of desks, chairs, and computers. They were aligned with four rows across. Each stretched down a long row of desks leading down to the far end of the large office where Farrell was standing. There was a good distance of cover for Tanner to get near Farrell without him knowing he was there. The long row of desks near Tanner was the furthest away from the windows and Farrell. With no lights shining on the floor, the police lights lighting up the building outside were the only light coming through. Being darker than it would be, Tanner knew he had a good chance of reaching Farrell and the hostages unseen.

Keeping himself low to the ground with his gun ready in hand, Tanner started his slow, quiet approach. Farrell was a crazed, thin, red-headed freak of a man. Shouting abuse out of the window. Still holding a large gun in his hand.

'We'll have a good time tonight. All the sexy little girls will be lining up for what I can offer them. Hey, down there. I'm still here. Alive and kicking.' Farrell fired a few more shots out of the window down onto the police.

Stopping his gunfire, he continued shouting, 'You're fighting to grab back the power of this city. But I know a man who gives me free rein. Free rein to screw every little girl I find. Before I fist a load of bullets in her skull.'

Tanner heard what Farrell had said. Just then, Tanner had spotted two dead teenage girls on the floor under one of the windows. A gunshot wound in each of their heads. Noticeably, having had their clothes ripped and torn apart from them, showing bare skin with both pairs of the teenager's legs spread wide open.

Tanner knew Farrell loved to rape them first, shoot them in the head. Then rape again the dead corpse.

You sick bastard, Tanner thought.

Full of anger and disgust, Tanner reached the last table at the far end of the row. The last table he could easily stay hidden from Farrell's view. He watched Farrell lean against the open window.

Pointing his gun down towards the office floor.

Looking around the edge of the table, Tanner could see another girl sat quietly on the office floor. With her back to him, he could not see her face. He could see that her body was shaking. He could hear she was breathing heavily. He knew she was terrified. Farrell now turned his gun on her.

'So, princess,' Farrell said. 'You're very pretty. Very beautiful. Very sexy. You saw what I did to your friends. Now it's your turn. And you're gonna love it. Take off your clothes. Or I'll make you. Do it now!'

Just then, Tanner accidentally banged his shoulder against the desk. Farrell heard it. He pointed his gun in Tanner's direction. Now standing up straight, he slowly took a few paces and headed towards the desk.

'Well, princess. Someone wants to join our special party. Come on out. If you don't, princess here won't get the pleasure of having me in her. Instead, she'll just get the bullet in her head.'

Farrell now aimed his gun at the girl's head. He could see no movement behind the desk.

'You're really pushing your luck, my friend,' Farrell spoke, full of frustration and anger.

Now, Tanner gave up. He rose up from the table. With his gun in hand, he placed his hands above his head.

'Tanner. You prick. Throw the gun away,' Farrell commanded.

Tanner threw away his gun towards the middle row of desks. The girl turned her head to where she heard the gun landing. Then she looked back at the gun Farrell had pointed at her. Farrell now gave his next order.

'Come towards me, Frank.'

Tanner walked slowly up to Farrell. When he was right in

26

Farrell's face, Farrell moved his gun away from the girl and used it to whack Tanner hard in the face. The hit made Tanner fall to the floor. Spitting blood out of his mouth.

'That's for getting on my nerves following me all these weeks.'

'You sick freak. You raped and murdered all those girls,' Tanner shouted as he looked up at Farrell.

In reply, Farrell kicked Tanner hard again and again in the stomach. 'Freak? I'm the freak? Everybody has to have a hobby, Frank.'

Farrell then lowered down and punched Tanner hard in the face over and over again. 'The princess is my next big meal today. Aren't you a sexy girl?'

Farrell heard nothing. No reply from the teenage girl. He turned to see her. But she was not there.

He instantly stood up and looked down the long stretch of office. All he saw were the chairs, computers and desks. No sign of the girl.

'Oh, princess. Do we have to play this game?'

Farrell started to walk down one aisle with desks left and right of him. Looking either side to see where the girl was hiding. Pointing his gun ahead of him. The office was now more silent. Tension in the air had risen in seconds. Farrell moved more into the middle of the office.

'There's no point hiding away in the shadows. In the dark. Come out and show your true colours, princess.'

Just then, the girl jumped out and grabbed hold of Farrell's gun. She punched Farrell hard in the face with another gun. Tanner's gun. She found it, remembering how distant the echo was of the gun banging a nearby desk. The force she hit Farrell's face with made Farrell lose grip of his gun as it dropped to the ground. The hit made him being pushed back several paces. Falling down to the floor.

The girl, now baring deep anger in her eyes at Farrell, stood above him as she spoke, 'I'm not your princess. I'm Jade.'

Instantly, Jade started hitting and kicking Farrell all over his body with her feet and fists. Farrell becoming more dazed with every hit.

Nearby, Tanner watched on in amazement as he picked himself up off the floor. Keeping well back as the fighting continued. Seeing Jade be relentless and full of force. She was beating the hell out of Farrell. Hitting his face, stomach, ribs and chest. Jade slowed down until she had stopped entirely. Still holding Tanner's gun, she aimed the gun at Farrell's head. Ready to blow his brains out.

'For all you've done to my friends and those other girls. You raped them and killed them. This is for them.'

Quickly, Tanner walked up to Jade. 'Don't do this,' Tanner said.

'You don't understand,' she replied. 'He made me watch him. Seeing him rape them, watching them cry, and blowing their brains out. And he laughed all the time.'

'Please, don't become like him and be a murderer.'

'Why? I'm an orphan. My parents were taken from me by a murderer. Now my friends are dead. There's nothing more I can lose now.'

'Yes, there is. You can lose the chance to live and move on. Trust me, please. You're not alone. People lose many things, many loved ones and many friends. But they also learn to get back up. And they don't let the loss eat away at who they are and make them become something they're not. You're not the same as him you're pointing the gun at. You have to be better than him.'

'You're saying all this to save Farrell?' Jade asked.

'No. I'm doing this to save you. To stop you from letting him win. This is what he wants. Please. Let me help you.'

Taking in what Tanner said, Jade began to cry and slowly lowered down her gun from Farrell. Tanner walked towards her. She handed over the gun to him. As he grabbed it, Jade collapsed, holding Tanner tight in her arms. Crying hard into his chest. Tanner also grabbed hold of Jade.

'It's okay everything's fine,' he said in comfort.

From outside, Tanner could hear the police begin to storm the building. Jade let go of him. She looked up at his eyes. She could see there was trust and care behind Tanner's eyes. Suddenly, she came over, all calm and relaxed.

'Thank you for what you did, Jade. It was very brave what you did.'

'Jade Hall. That's my name.'

'I'm Frank Tanner. Private Detective.'

Chapter 3

In the days to come, Farrell was arrested, put on trial, and placed in jail to serve a lifetime sentence.

Jade, meanwhile, was helped and supported to return to the orphanage she had grown up in. In the room she slept in, there were now two empty beds that once belonged to her two murdered friends. In the coming days, Jade slept very little. She kept her eyes on both those beds. Thinking of nothing but the memories and friendships she had had that were now gone.

Then came the toughest day. The saddest day of all. Jade was getting dressed in formal black-coloured clothing. Staring at herself in the mirror. Preparing herself for her two friends' funeral.

As she looked on, staring deep into her reflection, she quietly gave herself a few words of support.

Be strong and do it for them, she thought to herself. Now ready and prepared, she left the room.

*

A few hours later, the funeral service had now arrived at Southern Cemetery. Two coffins being led by a priest leading the service to two gravesides. Jade followed the coffins from behind. Apart from her and a handful of staff from the orphanage, no one else was present at the funeral.

As the coffins reached the graveside, with the priest saying his final words of the service, Jade turned to look at a nearby tree about a hundred feet away. She could see a person standing under the tree in the shadow, but she could not make out who it was.

She saw the person take a few steps forward. Stepping out from under the tree was Tanner. He was there to show his respect and support for Jade. Seeing him nearby reassured her. Yet she understood why Tanner was keeping his distance from the service. This was Jade's moment to say goodbye to her friends. He did not want to disrupt an important moment for her.

As the coffins had been lowered, the priest and staff moved away from the two open graves. Leaving Jade alone to be with her friends one last time. But Tanner stayed where he was. Not moving or walking away. In his mind, he had made a choice.

This girl has no one else to tum to, he thought. *I have to be there for her.*

*

Later that day, Jade had returned to the orphanage. She stood in the canteen looking out of a window down onto a field of trees and grass. It was silent. She was alone by herself with her thoughts.

Suddenly, at the far end, the door to enter the canteen opened. Jade looked to see Tanner walk through the door.

'I didn't mean to disturb you,' he said.

'I'd like some company,' she replied. 'I don't have much chance for that now my friends are gone.' Jade turned to look back out of the window.

Tanner started walking towards her slowly.

'How long have you lived here?' Tanner asked.

'Since I can remember.'

'You said your parents were murdered. Did they ever catch who did it?'

'No. Given the chance, I'd love to find him.'

'You fought well against Farrell. I was impressed.'

'This place taught me how to fend for myself.'

'You've got a lot of strength. And you say you'd want justice. Would you like these qualities to be nurtured?'

Tanner stopped walking and Jade now turned to look him face to face. 'What do you mean?' she asked.

'You know the police have different aims now. They aim to keep the peace. Not solve crimes. They don't give the right justice to the victims, their families, and their friends. That's my job. To help others where I can. I think you'd want to do the same.'

'What makes you think that?'

'Because of the justice that wasn't given to you. Would you want the same fate on another innocent persons' life?'

Jade nodded her head for no.

'Then let me help you, Jade. Let me train you and guide you to be a private detective like me.'

Tanner took a card out of his pocket with a contact number on it. He handed it over to Jade and she took it.

'Think about it, please. The offer is open whenever you're ready.'

With the offer given, Tanner turned and walked back towards the entrance at the far end. But he did not reach it before Jade asked one more question.

'Why would you do this for me?'

Tanner stopped walking once he heard the question. He turned and looked back at Jade. He knew he had to give the most honest answer to let Jade believe in him and trust him.

32

'Because I believe there's someone unique inside you. Someone who needs to grow beyond that of an orphan child. Become more than what she's seen to be. You have a chance to be that what drives you most. It's up to you whether you take it or not. So, think about it, Jade. Just think about it. This isn't the last time you'll see me; I'll be around from time to time. You just take care of yourself, Jade.'

With that, Tanner continued his walk. Leaving Jade alone once again in the canteen. Leaving her with her thoughts. Thoughts that were now very different to the ones she had the last time she was alone minutes earlier.

She looked down at the contact card she held in her hand. Thinking to herself, *Which choice should l make?*

Chapter 4

The choice Jade made was to focus on getting an education. Focusing hard and solid in the coming years towards getting her A-levels. Studying at Xaverian College.

From there, graduating up to studying for a degree in criminology at Alpha University. Proud of her achievement on her education, the subjects chosen in her studies proved that she had paid close attention to the advice Tanner had given her years before. Studying in fine detail the law, criminal justice, and lists of famous historical crimes, like Ian Brady and Myra Hindley, Doctor Harold Shipman, the terrorist bombings in Alpha City in 1992, 1996 and 2017.

But for Jade, university was not just all about degrees and education. It was here that Jade met a young man the same age as her. A man called Christian Torr. A slim-built, good-looking young man who had a love for athletic sports, boozing having fun with his gang of mates. At university, he was studying towards a career in politics. A poison chalice of a career thought Jade. But she was intrigued by Christian, mainly by how she saw two sides of his personality.

When Christian was alone with her, his sensitive, romantic side would show through. Jade being the centre of his attention. Making Jade feel like the centre of his whole world. Over time, she came to trust Christian. Letting down her guard. Opening up to him, she was falling in love with him. This side of Christian was who she loved most.

The other side of Christian was who she saw when he was with his mates. Hearing conversations about money, football, and shallow views of women. Seeing females as trophies. Also, sharing a rather shallow view of life overall. *Was this the real Christian,* Jade thought. *Or was he just falling in line with the groups' antics?* Selling away a part of himself so he was accepted and embraced by the group as a whole.

Jade's opinion of his friends was not good. Feeling they all had a bad influence on Christian. She wondered why men like this felt they needed to be this way to be accepted. Why was it important to degrade others, mainly women, to feel good about themselves and make them feel superior to them? These were a group of lads who found it hard to be an individual and could only function fully as a whole when they were part of a group.

Despite this flaw in Christian and his friends, he remained loyal to Jade during this period. They continued to develop their relationship to the point that they moved in together and were now officially a couple.

With their love and relationship blossoming, both Jade and Christian graduated from Alpha University. Many a night would end with both embracing each other, lying naked on top of their bed. Making love with passionate expression.

After Christian had fallen asleep on these nights, Jade would lie awake looking at his face.

Knowing she was with the love of her life. The man who was her life. And she knew that to be the truth.

Jade felt so secure and confident of her future life with Christian. She had been given no reason not to. He treated her well and as an equal. An important point for Christian as he was aiming to take that into his political career.

Christian really loved Jade. He thought her to be the most

beautiful woman he had ever seen, both inside and out. A woman who brought him out of his laddish, cultured shell. Making him blossom into more of a man and a lover than he was capable of doing on his own.

All Christian wanted in his life was Jade. Nothing more or less than that. Anything more would bring vulnerability and insecurity to Christians' life. Something he could not afford to have when aiming for a long career in politics. He aspired to have it with as much focus and attention on that goal.

As for what was to come would not bring a shared reaction with the same feelings. But rather that of two people reacting in two very different ways.

Jade announced she was pregnant. And she could not have been any happier. Unplanned as it was, Jade embraced this miracle as something to be cherished.

For Christian, it built up uncertainty about himself and his abilities. He made it plain he was not happy nor comfortable with the idea of becoming a father. He did not want to be a parent. He had personal ambitions beyond that of living in Alpha City. He feared being a father would become a shackle in his life. Holding him back on having his personal freedom and on his aspirations of becoming a strong political leader.

In the days following her announcement, Jade and Christian's differences were beginning to widen them further apart from each other. Arguments and rows started to escalate. Even becoming heated. To the point that Christian demanded Jade to have an abortion. This was the moment Jade passionately said no. She was keeping the baby no matter what.

For Christian, this was the point of no return. Fearful of becoming a parent. Not wanting to face up to the responsibility, Christian had made up his mind.

One night, when Jade was fast asleep, Christian quietly got up out of bed. He packed up his belongings, left the flat and drove off in his car, leaving Jade behind alone in the flat. Never to come back.

The next morning, Jade woke to realise the other half of the bed was empty. Walking through all the rooms in the flat, Jade was now physically showing a large bump from her pregnancy, which was now at seven months. Knowing Christian was not in the flat, she thought to look in the wardrobe and cupboards. With all of Christian's clothes gone; the reality now hit home for Jade.

He's done it. He's gone, she thought.

Jade was heartbroken. She could feel her heart being crushed by what he had done. Full of emotion, she started to cry. Whilst simultaneously rubbing her hand gently across her pregnant self. Both maternally comforting her unborn child and also comforting herself whilst doing it. Being a mother in waiting.

She was now alone to parent a child she knew was precious and special. She knew, unlike Christian, it was nothing to be shameful about. She knew the times ahead would be difficult as a lone parent. But she would not let that set her back. She aimed to give her child the best childhood she could possibly give. A child she already knew was more important to her than anyone else alive.

Yes, Christian has left and he should be ashamed of himself, thought Jade, *for making our child now grow up without a father.* But Jade knew she would not let their child be set back because of that.

Jade was determined to make her child be the best he or she could possibly be. And by doing so, she was focused on being the best mother she could be for her unborn child.

Chapter 5

Jade was lying across a hospital bed. Sat upright, screaming in pain with her legs wide open. She had gone into labour. Nurses surrounded her bed. Advising and supporting her through the process. It had now been lasting a couple of hours. Jade, exhausted and fatigued, was shouting at the top of her lungs as she pushed hard. Tears streaming down her face.

Outside the delivery room in the corridor stood Tanner. Watching through a glass window. He looked on nervously and concerned for both Jade and the baby. He could hear her screams even with him standing in the corridor. Also heard were the faint sounds of the nurses giving support to Jade. Seeing her push harder and harder. Her screams became louder and louder.

Then came the first cry of Jade's baby. Tanner could see the baby. Being cleaned and wrapped in a blanket by a nurse. Jade collapsed back on her bed when it was all over. She felt tired and overjoyed at the same time as the nurse handed over Jade's baby to her.

Tanner smiled, full of joy. He could see Jade holding her baby in her arms. Looking down at her child's face. Gently holding her child's hands in hers. Then he saw Jade begin to cry. They were tears of joy. She was now a mother. And it was the best feeling in the world to have.

*

Sometime later, Jade and her baby were now in their own private hospital room. Jade rested in bed with her eyes closed. Her baby was in a cot placed by the side of her bed. Both of them calm, peaceful and tranquil.

Just then, Jade heard the door to her room gently and quietly open. She opened her eyes to see who was coming in. It was Tanner. Once he saw Jade was awake, he started to leave.

'Sorry. I didn't mean to wake you,' he said.

'No. Wait. Frank. Please stay,' Jade said.

Tanner walked quietly in. Gently closing the door. He walked over to Jade. Gently grabbing hold of her hand, Tanner looking on her very proud.

'You did really good, Jade. You should be proud of yourself.'

'I am.'

Tanner walked round the bed to take a look at the baby in the cot, who was at peace and fast asleep. 'Is it a boy or a girl?' he asks.

'A boy,' replied Jade.

'He's beautiful. When the nurses saw me in the corridor, they kept asking me to come into the room. I think they thought I was your father or your child's father. You never said where the father was.'

'I don't know where Christian is. He left us. I want to thank you, Frank.'

'Why?'

'For stepping in. Supporting me when I had no one else to turn to.'

'I'll support you all the way, Jade, whether that be financially or as a friend. Whatever it is, I'll be here for you.'

'Thank you. You don't know how much that means to me.

But all I want to be right now is a great mother to my little boy.'

'Have you thought of a name yet?'

'Sean. His name is Sean.'

*

And so, in the weeks and months ahead, Jade gave all her time and attention to Sean. She could not be any happier doing it. Bathing him, clothing him, feeding him, taking him for walks around the local park, celebrating his first birthday, then his second and then his third. Time was flying by for both of them. For Jade, it was as if the world had disappeared. For her, her life was being a mother to her son Sean.

And then came Sean's first day at school. Dressed smartly in his uniform, Sean was full of excitement at making new friends. Then the school bell rang. Jade hugged Sean one last time before letting him go.

As she did, Jade had a tear for having to let go of Sean. Letting him go and start a new beginning in nursery school. A new beginning for Sean.

And now Sean was at school, Jade now had the time to turn her attention to Tanner's offer she had been given many years before. An offer she felt ready to take him up on. She felt her time had come. She took out of her wallet the contact card Tanner gave her back at the orphanage. She had kept it all this time. It read:

'FRANK TANNER. PRIVATE DETECTIVE. 68 DALE STREET. ALPHA CENTRAL.'

Chapter 6

Walking down Dale Street, Jade reached the address and opened the door. Walking up the staircase to the top floor, she walked down a long, varnished floor corridor. With blinds drawn down on windows to her right and a row of doors to empty rooms to her left, she reached a specific door with Tanner's name engraved on it. From inside the room, she could hear a conversation taking place. She knocked on the door.

'Come in,' she heard Tanner say from inside the room. With that, Jade opened the door and walked in.

In the office, Jade saw Tanner sat behind his desk. He was talking to a young black police officer who was sat down, but out of respect, stood up once he saw Jade enter the room.

The young officer was dressed well in a suit, tie, thin build, clean shaven with a fresh, clean look to him. This was a man who, in Jade's eyes, seeing him for the first time, looked very handsome. She appreciated how respectful he was at standing up to her entering the room.

Tanner, meanwhile, looked happily surprised to see Jade. He stood up but more slowly got up out of his chair.

'Jade, it's good to see you,' Tanner said.

'You too, Frank,' replied Jade.

'What brings you here?'

Jade took out of her coat pocket the card Tanner had given her. She went and placed it on his desk.

'I wanted to take you up on the offer you gave me several

years ago.'

'I'm pleased you think that way, Jade.'

Tanner noticed her turning her attention to the young officer. Implying she would like to be introduced to him.

'Jade, this is Louis Walker. An officer in Julius Carvers' police unit.'

'It's a pleasure to meet you, Miss Hall,' Louis said.

'Call me Jade.'

Jade and Louis shook hands. As they did, she looked back at Tanner to ask him a question. 'Are the police wanting to solve crimes again and not just keep the peace? Is that the reason you're here, Louis?' Jade asked.

'Louis is willing to be a contact and friend within the unit for me,' Tanner replied.

'Don't you mean he's a contact and friend within the unit for us, Frank?' Jade asked.

Tanner understood what Jade was telling him now. He understood he now had a new partner in his office.

'Yes, Jade. You're right,' Tanner said.

'Well, I'd better be off,' said Louis.

Just then, Jade turned away from the two men and walked over to a shelf on the wall. As Tanner and Louis were saying the last bits of their conversation, Jade looked over casually at the few ornaments placed on the shelf. But then her eye got attracted to a photo frame placed on the shelf.

It was a photo of Tanner with his wife and son outside a countryside mansion on a clear summer day.

Interesting how he never mentions his family, thought Jade. *Where is his wife and son? Should I ask him? Probably not the right time.*

Just then, she turned away from the photo. Looking back

42

towards Louis and Tanner. As Louis left the room, both she and Tanner looked at the other.

'He seems a nice young man,' said Jade.

'I knew his father. Louis has a lot of his qualities in him. He's honest, decent, and loyal. But Jade, as you're here, I guess you have a few questions for me?'

'Only one. When do I start?'

*

In the days and weeks to come, Jade put herself into training a regime that would get her ready for the job.

Ranging from exercising her fitness fully at the gym, running and jogging through parks, going to a local gun training facility. Training her eye and sharpness at shooting whoever was to be her target. Then, training to be a boxer and a fighter. Holding her own fighting men of all sizes. At all times remaining sharp, focused, and becoming physically fit to do the job she most wanted to do.

The early jobs given to her consisted of getting her feet comfortable in the job. Ranging from who had staged robberies, stealing valuable items from vulnerable people. Tracking them down. Finding them, fighting them. Beating them to a pulp. Bringing them to a police station. Giving justice to the victims returning their valuables.

Other jobs have her fighting for her life with men. The type of men who thought women were a walkover, who were beneath them and their abilities. Underestimating Jade, her abilities, and her power as a strong, independent woman.

There were other jobs given that were more delicate. Such as infidelity. Suspicions from a wife about her husband. Jade having to follow the husband through the night. Seeing where he goes and who he meets. Following him to a private hotel room. She would take photos of his sexual intercourse with his new lover, prostitute or whoever took his fancy that night.

Once developing the photos, she would report back to the wife. And with regret, report back with the photos of what the trail had led her to. Even though it hurt, Jade knew the truth was more important than the fantasy that everything was still okay.

Chapter 7

Sometimes, there were cases that fell into her lap from no client and no new case. They came from Jade acting on instinct alone. Because she knew it was the right thing to do.

One night, Jade was starting to leave the offices on Dale Street. Walking down the street, heading for home to a block of flats in Alpha Central. The heavens had opened heavy with rain tonight. Jade, not having a hood attached to her long black coat or having an umbrella on her person, had started becoming soaked through. Her long black-haired streaks now weighed heavy down from her head.

As she walked, her eyes were attracted to flashing lights coming from across the street down a side alley called Lizard Street, just off Dale Street. A police cordon was placed on the end of the alley, meeting the main road with police cars and officers already at the scene.

Curious to know more, Jade crossed the road to stand by the police line, where an officer stood on guard. The officer saw her approaching.

'There's nothing to see here, Miss. It's all over,' the officer said.

'I'm a private detective. What happened here?' Jade asked.

'There's been a murder on one of the homeless from Alphaville. The murderer was gone before we got here.'

'Where's the body?'

'Back at the morgue. We're just cleaning up the scene and then getting back to our main job.'

'Someone's died. Don't you care about his family and friends wanting to know what happened?' Jade asked.

'He's homeless. No fixed address. We didn't put him on the streets. He chose to live that way. We wipe our hands off them.'

Jade looked disappointed at the response from the officer. Then she saw a young man. About nineteen years old, sat on the floor of the alley nearby.

'Who's the young man?' Jade asked.

'He's called Luke Goddard,' the officer replied. 'Another one of the homeless from Alphaville. He was a friend of the murdered man. He was here when we got here.'

'I'd like to talk to him.'

'Be my guest.'

Jade walked towards the young man called Luke. As she approached, he looked up at her. Jade could not tell where Luke's tears stopped and where the rain on his face started running down.

Luke was homeless and lived in an area of the city centre called Alphaville. A place originally known as Alpha City Gardens; it had been turned into a shelter village community for the homeless to live in without fear of attack. A place for the homeless to go to when there was nowhere else to go. The roots of this community go as far back as the Great Depression in the U.S in the 1930s called Hooverville, where similar villages were found all across the country named after the then President Hoover.

For the next few minutes, Jade consoled the young Luke. Wanting to know more about him and his murdered friend.

Luke was smart. Fending for himself, living tough on the

streets. Protecting both he and the others in Alphaville from the crimes and troubles to be found in the city.

Luke was a slim teenager who knew how to handle himself when the going got tough. Recently, his instincts had taught him how it was important to look after the youngsters in Alphaville. It brought out his qualities as a leader and a protector. Even bringing out some paternal instincts towards the younger homeless kids on the streets.

But tonight still showed how vulnerable he was. By finding the body of a young man aged sixteen. A youngster who had come to Luke for support. With his death, Luke had become deeply affected by not being able to protect the young man from murder. He felt he had failed in his role guiding the younger homeless kids.

Crying into his hands, his eyes were bloodshot red. He was helpless, broken and needed some comfort of hope.

Seeing Jade was that hope. As she sat by him, listening to all he said, he knew there was a comfort to Jade as a person. A quality that made him open up to her. Jade, being a mother, knew how to be that way. But she knew there had to be more to her than that. She could see a young man heartbroken at the loss of a friend he cared so much about. Jade knew she had to do something.

After several minutes, Jade had made up her mind. She was going to find the murderer. Not for money or her profession. But knowing she had to because it was the right thing to do for Luke.

Jade swore and promised Luke that she would catch the killer. And in that moment, he heard a passionate conviction in Jade's voice. It made him think that he could trust her and he believed she would do it.

For the next few days, Luke stayed within the confines of Alphaville. His confidence and self-belief had taken a knock. As he looked out into the city streets at night time, he knew the dark city shadows were where the real crimes took place. Staying hidden and out of view. He knew the criminals would hide out in the shadows until the time was right.

With this being the case, he knew the city centre lights were a safe haven for him. But only for so long.

Tonight, Luke dared to leave Alphaville. Now, sat alone on the ground near the entrance to Alpha Central Train Station. The glassy entrance shone enough light out to give Luke the comfort of being safe, at least for now. He sat alone, begging in the street. Hoping for anyone to give him some change to take back to the village.

Later, he knew he would have to go back to check up on the other homeless people living in Alphaville, both young and old. Checking on their health, their well-being and seeing if they are comfortable enough to get a good night's sleep. Being in this role, Luke was beginning to step up as a potential leader within Alphaville. Even being nineteen years old, he was stepping up to be a father figure to the youngsters who had no parents in their lives. As well as being respected by the elders living in the village.

But who did Luke have? Who could he turn to for help whenever he needed it and give his support back in return?

'They told me I'd find you here,' a familiar female voice said. Luke looked up to see Jade smiling, holding a cardboard box. 'This is for you and the rest. Take it,' she said.

He stood up to grab the box. It felt heavy.

'I got you some food and drink for all of you. I thought you should celebrate.'

'Why?' Luke asked.

'I found the guy who murdered your friend.'

Luke was happily shocked at what he just heard. His face came alive with happy surprise.

'Thank you, Jade,' he gratefully said.

'Anytime you need my help or support, I'm here for you and your friends,' Jade said. 'Come on. I'll give you a lift to your friends with this. It's about time you all had a good night together.'

Jade and Luke walked away together towards her car. Jade was feeling proud of herself inside. It was moments like this she did it for. This was why she wanted this job. To give justice. Her only wish was that someone could give that to her in regard to the murder of her parents. To catch the one responsible for their deaths. But knowing she would not wish that on others, Jade had done her good deed for Luke. *A* deed that could finally give him peace of mind and heart.

*

A few hours later, Jade stood alone on top of a high city centre building, looking down on a lit-up Alpha City at night. The spectacle of the city was so beautiful for Jade to look down upon.

Standing tall, physically fit, thin built, her long black hair swayed gently in the night wind. So did her long black coat. Covering over her clothing of a white formal shirt, tight black jeans, wearing small black leather-heeled boots.

After all the training, exercising and early assignments given to her, Jade was now moulded into the image and person she aspired to be. She knew it as she remembered the words in her mind that Tanner had said to her earlier that day.

'Jade, we serve those who need help. We're there for them when there's no one else to tum to. We will help protect the people and the city. And we won't choose emotion over thought in our judgement of the criminals. I feel you're ready to serve them now. You're ready to be given the title. You are now Private Detective Jade Hall.'

Chapter 8

Julius Carver was regaining consciousness. But still only half awake to know exactly what was happening. His sight was pitch black. He could feel fabric touching his face. He slowly grew aware that his head was fully covered over with a black sack. No light shone through, helping him know where he was. He could feel two strong hands. Each holding a strong grip on each of his arms.

Dragging him forcefully. Not letting Julius get a footing for himself to walk.

Julius could hear the echo of their footsteps fall away far and wide into the distance. *Where am I,* thought Julius. *A warehouse? A stadium?*

Suddenly, the two-armed men dragging Julius slammed him down hard on the seat of a chair. The echo of the chair slamming on the ground reverberated around the unknown surroundings Julius was in. He could hear the flapping of a bird's wings. Still, with the sack over his face, Julius could not make out many other sounds. The dripping of water falling down from a leaking roof. Gently falling down into a puddle within the building he was now in.

How did I get here? Julius thought.

*

Only an hour or two before, Julius was sat behind his desk at police headquarters. Finishing up the last of his work tonight. Being one of the last to leave the offices before heading home. He was looking over the files of recent cases and dealings with associates of businessman and mob leader Jack Kane. Wanting to go deeper into studying how Kane rose to so strong a prominence over the course of the past twenty years. Looking over how he was able to grab a hold of dominance and power on the city. To the point that the police and local government had no alternative but to appease the powerful businessman. To study all the files had spanned over the past few weeks. Julius now had a better understanding of Jack Kane.

Feeling tired and exhausted, Julius chose to finally call it a night. He decided to pick up where he left off in the morning. It had been a long day at the police headquarters. But Julius liked it like that as he was so professionally driven. All that waited for Julius at home was a drink and an empty house. At the moment, he had no time for a love life or family life. He was driven by his ambitions for bigger and better things down the line. All these qualities were encouraged to him by his father.

Julius' father had been his role model. The image of who to be and who he aspired to be. A good man with a good heart. Someone who expanded his love onto Julius' former friend Frank Tanner.

I hope my dad's okay, thought Julius. *I should go see him again. It would help lift him up. He's been in hospital for so long. This condition has taken its toll on him. When I get the time, I'll be there for him.*

When alone, Julius' thoughts drifted back and forth between his father and Tanner, his former friend. Two boys who grew up together. So close. Almost like brothers. Then came the split that ended it all. Dividing them both. Making them go down two very different paths. The ties of friendship no longer there.

Yet, inside Julius, there was still the smallest seed of care inside Julius for Tanner. For the man he once was. For the friend he once was.

But Julius must shake those thoughts of conflict within him. It was now all in the past. All gone now. But yet so hard to forget the memories.

Leaving the headquarters by himself, Julius made his way towards his car in the police headquarters car park. The area was dark and quiet. Only a row of thin, long strips of fluorescent light shone up the area. Julius walked along cautiously. He knew at night that a car park was a place of shadows and mystery. Looking around him, beyond the area lit up, he could see nothing but darkness. The light fades into the pitch dark of night. The car park still contained an eerie quality to it. You never knew if you were truly by yourself or not.

And tonight, Julius would know he was not alone. Ahead of him, stepping out of the dark into the light, were two tall, bald, muscular men. Julius stopped walking once he saw them. He turned to look behind him. Now, there were two more men there of a similar build. The four men moved to circle around Julius. He was now trapped.

'What do you all want?' Julius asked the men. None of them replied.

Suddenly, from behind, Julius felt the whack of metal hit the back of his head. He fell down to the floor. Knocked unconscious from the hit.

*

Now sat in the chair, still with the black sack covering his head,

Julius felt a hand grab hold of the sack. Pulling it off his head. Finally, Julius saw his surroundings for the first time. Seeing who removed the black sack from his head. It was Tyson. Kane's second in command.

A muscular, black man in his late thirties who looked up to Kane as a leader and figurehead he himself aspired to be. With Kane in his mid-fifties, Kane considered Tyson to be the obvious candidate to take over his business in the future at some point. Even at an early age, Kane saw similar qualities in Tyson that he once had. The only thing Tyson needed from Kane was the guidance of leadership.

Up ahead, Julius saw two car headlamps shining directly at him. Making it hard for Julius to see clearly. As he turned his head away from the headlamps, he saw standing on either side of him two of the tall, bald men who kidnapped him. Beyond them, he could see he was in a large warehouse. All dark apart from the side warehouse windows. Shining moonlight from outside down onto the concrete floor of the warehouse. Looking up above, he saw the rusted holes and gaps in the ceiling roof. Seeing the water dripping and the birds flying. Julius looked around for clues to know where he was. But he had no idea where he had been taken to.

Then suddenly, Julius heard the sound of a car door open and then slammed shut. He turned to look back at the car headlamps. He saw an unseen person stand in front of him. Causing a long shadow to expand along the large stretch of concrete floor. As the person walked up to Julius, he became more visible to him. Standing there was the ominous, powerful figure of Jack Kane.

Dressed neat, clean, business-like with a slim build. Wearing a black suit, black tie with grey hair gelled back. Here was the businessman and leader of the city mob.

Staring down at Julius, he quietly spoke.

'You asked my men, what did they want? Mister Carver. It's simple. I want you,' Kane calmly said.

'Why?' Julius asked.

'You know who I am, don't you, Julius?'

'All too well. You got a lot of balls to kidnap a police officer. That was part of the deal you struck with the police and the mayor's office. You wouldn't kidnap or murder official figures.'

'Yes. That deal. The one so the police could keep the peace for the city as a whole. The one that had you give up Alpha Central and my agreement to stay within that boundary.'

'The police had no choice but to make that deal,' Julius replied. 'Giving you the central point of the city. It was either that or let you overthrow the police, and the local government. We all know you have the manpower for that.'

'So, the police went into business with me and opted for the lesser of two evils. Is that what you're saying, Julius?'

Julius gave no reply.

'Well, I've got some news for you,' Kane said. 'I'm a businessman. Expansion is inevitable.'

'So, what's all this then you bringing me here? A threat? A warning?'

'No. It's an opportunity. For you, Julius.'

Julius burst out laughing at the absurd gesture.

'This is not a joke,' Kane said. 'This is an opportunity to play with the big boys. And it's all summed up in one name. Farrell. The modern-day Jack the Ripper locked up in your cells.'

'A padded cell, you mean? Where he'll be for the rest of his life.'

'Ah. So, he's a priority case?' Kane asked.

'What do you expect for the killings he did?'

'I'll tell you what I expect. I expect a fresh partnership with a man on the inside. That man being you, Julius. You see, I've done deals with your prisoner Farrell in the past.'

'Meaning?'

'Meaning I'm willing to do business with the man who put him there as well. I'm told you like to have an eye on the big prize. Yes?'

Kane turned to Tyson. He took from him a wad of cash notes. Holding them, Kane held them in front of Julius' face.

'What will it be, Julius? How much will it take?'

Staring at the cash notes, Julius pondered on the offer. But he was not convinced. He was curious to know more.

'Why do you want Farrell?' Julius asked. 'What's he to you?'

'Let's just say he makes a good cocktail in the kitchen,' replied Kane. 'He might be mad. But he's also a chemist for anarchy and chaos.'

'Why should I help you?'

'Because I know your dirty little secrets. Your secrets of how you really got your position. How you really became head of the Alpha Central Division? I know you're a man of ambition. That's why you cut ties with your former friend Frank Tanner.'

'I cut my ties with Frank because he lost control of his life and his profession. And it cost him.'

'That's the story you'll stick to. Using Tanner as an excuse. But we both know how you tick. And we know what talks more to you. You just have to look at the big picture.'

'And what's that Kane?'

'The final frontier for hopes and dreams lies in the corporate hands of the businessman. He's the one who's able to keep on dreaming. Everybody else is being dreamed by corporate businesses. Everyone is a tool of the corporate machine. Consuming new trends, new ideas, new platforms. Blindly following like a herd for the sake of corporate profits. Think about that. Think what you could do with all that power and profit, Julius.'

Julius did not reply. He now thought harder than ever on Kane's offer.

Kane then spoke, 'You make sure that Farrell says nothing and that he won't be executed. And I give my word you'll be treated the same. After all, we both don't want the A.C.P.D to know about our little talk. Neither of us wants to see you dragged out of your office and position in the police in disgrace. Even though we both know you deserve to be. More than anyone else.'

Just then, Julius looked straight at the money in Kane's hand. Then Julius grabbed hold of it. Now, with Julius holding the money, he was now in business with Jack Kane.

'What exactly have you got in mind?' Julius asked.

'This is the plan,' Kane replied. 'And this is what you'll do.'

Chapter 9

Farrell lied back on his bed. Alone in his prison cell. Looking up at the ceiling. Pondering on the length of time he had spent locked up for his crimes. Days had become months, and months had become years. Thinking back to that young sexy bitch Jade. Farrell still yearned to put her in her place. Doing to her what he had done to her friends and other young, vulnerable women.

As he fantasised more about the act, the more erotically aroused he became. As sick and twisted as he was, it was the latter stages of his sexual criminal acts that turned him on. Even more than sexual intercourse would for the average person.

The prison cell was dark. Nighttime had fallen. The clear night sky outside gave the moon all the sky it needed to shine down on the city tonight. The light shone through the prison cell window and bars. Down onto the floor and wall facing opposite Farrell.

It was silent. All that was heard was Farrell's calm and paced breathing. He had grown accustomed to the silence that when the sound was disturbed, he would notice and instantly be sharp and alert.

Which is why Farrell turned his head on the pillow to the left. Looking towards the prison cell door at the far end of his cell. Hearing the footsteps of the prison warden for this cell block, slowly walking past Farrell's cell door outside in the corridor. Farrell heard the keys attached to the prison warden rattling with each step he made. With each footstep, Farrell heard the sound become more distant. And distant. And distant. Until it reached a faint echo.

Then, suddenly outside, Farrell heard several footsteps. Moving fast and quickly. The leather on the shoes squeaked along the cold, polished floor. Then, the sound of punching fists. Keys rattling fast and quick. Then, a loud crack of bone breaking. And then nothing.

Has someone killed the warden? Farrell questioned thoughtfully.

Just then, the sound of footsteps started getting louder and louder. Farrell, not taking his eye off the door, slowly rose up from his bed. He now sat on the edge of it. Feeling both excited and nervous. Yet not knowing who was outside his cell door holding the loud-sounding rattling keys.

The footsteps stopped outside Farrell's door. At the base of the door, Farrell saw the person outside make a shadow with their body. The person inserted the key into the door. Unlocking it. Farrell's face started to lift with a big smile.

As the door opened, the faint light from the corridor shone into the cell. Lighting it up instantly. Farrell stared at the person standing in the open doorway. A familiar face from years ago. But not in familiar attire. Instead, wearing the uniform of a prison officer, was Tyson. Standing there inviting Farrell to leave his cell.

Farrell now felt like a naughty little schoolboy. Smiling more and bigger with each second. Then suddenly, Farrell quietly spoke his first words to Tyson, 'It's time to come out and play with the little kiddies again.'

*

Jack Kane sat quietly in the back seat of a parked car. Wearing his long black coat smoking a cigar. Looking at his watch, he looked up ahead out of the front car window. Looking past his driver, who sat there still and quiet.

The car was parked alongside the street path that ran directly along the prison Farrell was kept in.

Strangeways Prison.

Noticing the night was peaceful and calm, he sat back comfortably and continued to smoke his thick cigar.

*

Inside the prison, Julius was alone. Now, in the main C.C.T.V control room. Watching a bank of monitors. Four on each row. Watching Tyson leading Farrell through the corridors. As they left, being seen on one monitor, they then appeared on another.

As Julius had helped Tyson get into the prison with the help of the uniform, Julius was readying himself to wipe the tapes for each monitor that had coverage of both Tyson and Farrell in them. Once completed, the plan was to make a cover story to explain his visit to the prison so late at night. And he would then make his way to the corridor outside Farrell's prison cell. Being the first officer on the scene to discover the dead police warden whose neck was broken by Tyson. And to be the first to know that Farrell had escaped. All he had to do was wait a good ten minutes after Farrell and Tyson had got clear of the prison in Kane's car.

All was going to plan. Julius noticed on the monitor Tyson undoing his police uniform shirt. Taking out explosives strapped around his stomach. Seeing Farrell and Tyson reach a wall, Julius looked on to see Tyson starting to attach the explosives to the wall. Inserting wires into each device. Then, connecting each wire to a small detonating box.

Suddenly, Julius became distracted. He had on him a police radio mic. The sound from it was loud.

It was the voice of Louis Walker. 'Sir, this is Louis. Can you hear me?'

Julius, still watching Tyson and Farrell on the monitor, spoke into his radio mic.

'Yes, Louis. I can hear you. What's up?'

'Sir. We've just had a report of Jack Kane being spotted near Strangeways Prison.'

Julius, now concerned, turned away from the monitor. Concerned the plan was now in jeopardy. 'Is that a confirmed report?' Julius asked.

'Confirmed, sir,' Louis replied. 'Sir, if he's outside the Alpha Central border, we could take him in on violation of treaty. I've got the men ready to take him in. All we need is your order, sir. So, do we have the order?'

Julius did not reply. He now pondered long and hard. *What should I do?* Julius thought. *Give the order, or be a marked man for breaking the deal? Do I risk being an enemy of Jack Kane's? But if I pull out of catching Kane, will it give rise to suggest I might be in allegiance with him?*

Julius knew those thoughts within the police would lead to a suspension and termination of his career he had worked so long and hard to build.

Julius had to make a choice. Slowly placing the radio mic up to his mouth. He still could not make the decision. Once more, Louis gave one last request for action.

'Sir, do we have the order?'

Chapter 10

BANG!

The effect from Tyson's explosives made a hole in the prison wall on ground level. Leading out onto the city street.

From inside his car, Kane sat up, having seen the explosion some hundred feet away up ahead of him. Kane gave an order to his driver.

'Start the engine.' The driver followed his command.

Up ahead, Tyson and Farrell stepped through the hole in the prison wall out onto the street. Tyson guided Farrell towards Kane's car. Walking at a fast pace, Tyson looked all around at the rest of the long, quiet, empty street. He felt satisfied they were alone.

Tyson opened the front passenger car door placed alongside the road. Farrell got in the front seat alongside the driver. Once inside, Farrell slammed the door shut. Tyson moved to the back seat door. Opening it, he got into the back seat. Looking over at Kane, Tyson gave him a confident look, suggesting that everything went to plan. Kane smiled back.

Just then, police cars stormed the street at both ends. Blocking any chance of escape. Quickly, police officers stormed out of their cars. Ready and armed, pointing directly at Kane's car.

Kane, Tyson, and Farrell looked back and forth at each end of the street. Looking out of the front and rear windows. Kane knew what had happened. And he knew who was responsible.

Julius, you bastard, Kane thought.

Standing by a police car nearby, pointing his gun, was Louis Walker. Being the most senior officer at the scene, he took command. Shouting orders towards the car.

'This is the police. You are under arrest for the violation of the Alpha Central treaty. Step out of the car. Now.'

With that, Tyson stepped out. He began slowly raising up his hands. As he did, Tyson grabbed hold of a large gun hidden strapped behind him on his back. Tyson started shooting ruthlessly towards the street end where Louis and the other officers were.

The officers retaliated. Tyson ducked down using the open car door for cover. Kane, inside the car, got out his gun and started shooting through the now shattered rear window. Smashing and breaking it open to get clear shots of the officers at the opposite end, giving cover for Tyson. Farrell, armless, ducked for cover. Whilst the driver, armed, started shooting out of his side window.

The night air was so loud. Alive with the sound of gunfire. Neither side giving up. Kane and Tyson reloaded their guns several times.

Tyson wasted no time. Shooting down several officers up ahead of him. Louis looked down at his fallen comrades. But he knew he must continue to fire.

Tyson now took a chance with some little insurance. He undid two explosives still strapped to his chest. Explosives that were spared had the prison explosion not worked first time. He now attached the wires to the explosives.

Kane watched him do this. Knowing what Tyson was going to do with them, Kane passed over his cigar towards Tyson. Catching it, Tyson lit up each wire. The explosives were now dynamite. The sparks now alight.

Tyson gave one long throw for the first explosive and then another throw for the second. Each explosive had reached the police cars at one end of the street.

Louis stopped shooting once noticing the explosives and gave a command to his officers nearby. 'Clear the cars now. Fire in the hole.'

Instantly, Louis and the officers ran far back from the cars. All police cars at their end of the street smashed and exploded with ferocity as the explosives lit up the night full of flames and fire.

Tyson took the chance. Jumping in the car, the driver sped fast towards the flaming, burning police cars. Putting his foot down, the driver smashed through two burning police cars. Pushing them apart. Causing another mini-explosion in each car. With the roadway clear ahead, Kane's car sped fast away into the night. Escaping the scene of the gunfire.

Nearby, Louis hopelessly stood back. Seeing the police cars from the other far end of the street beginning their pursuit of Kane's car. Driving through the opening of the burning police cars.

With them gone, all that remained at the scene were burning cars on fire, several officers, including Louis, alive, others wounded, others dead. Louis relayed back to Julius on his radio mic.

'Sir. Kane's got away. Officers are down and wounded. We have a pursuit in place. Standby for a further report. Over and out.'

*

Several hours later, Julius had now returned to his office. Standing and staring out of his window. Waiting for the next report to come in. Thinking back on the choice he had made to strike an attack at Kane. Backstabbing him like he did. An action that could still backfire in his direction. Julius had potentially covered his tracks with his business dealings with Kane. It all depended on the next report.

Suddenly, his phone office rang. He quickly walked to his desk and picked up his phone. Louis was on the other end.

'Yes?' Julius said.

'Sir, they got away,' Louis replied. 'They got back to Alpha Central. Once they crossed back into Kane's territory, we had to abandon the chase. We had no choice. We lost them.'

'Understood Louis.'

'Sir, I know we can't take him when he's in Alpha Central. But he broke the treaty. Isn't that just cause to find him and take him in?'

'No. The police can't afford to officially take that risk. That would mean mutual violation of the city treaty. With that, Kane would have the power to take us down. We'll let him go. Report back to H.Q and file your report.'

Julius placed the phone back down on the receiver.

He now knew he was in trouble. He now knew he was a potential marked man from Kane.

*

Kane was back in his main office. In a business office in a tall, high-rise building overlooking the whole city. He was already deep in conversation with Tyson and Farrell. Kane was remembering back to what Julius had done to him. Betraying him like he did.

He's got a lot of balls to do that, Kane thought of Julius. His eyes were full of rage. But yet he remained composed, decent, and calm.

'He'll pay for what he's done,' Kane said. 'He thought he'd grab us all in one single swoop? Looking like the big hero for this city? Well, he'll just have to wait and see when I have full control of the city. Then, I'll expose the real Julius Carver.'

'But, sir, they're onto us now we've crossed the treaty border,' Tyson said. 'What's stopping them doing the same?'

'Civil war,' replied Kane. 'That's why they wouldn't dare. The police can't afford to risk it for themselves. There's too much at stake for them. From now on, we must play the game very delicately. And it's only fair we hit back at them in our own way.'

Just then, Kane turned his focus towards Farrell. Farrell stood quiet, smiling at Kane. Kane walked over to Farrell, ready to give him his next command.

'I understand, Farrell, you've still got a taste for a particular Z-listed drug. And we all know you have a taste for the youth of this city. Tyson.'

Just then, Tyson walked over to Farrell. Handing him a list of names and families.

'Those names on there are a list of the most powerful families in the city,' Kane said. 'You strike at them, then you can help cripple the foundations of the city and who finances it. How does that sound to you, Farrell?'

'Well,' Farrell said, 'it looks like the naughty boy is ready to come out to play again.'

Chapter 11

The next morning, Jade and Tanner were being briefed by Louis in Tanner's office. Being given an update of the recent breakout of Farrell from prison. Both Jade and Tanner were giving their full attention to what Louis had to say.

'We kept on their tail as far as we could. Once they crossed the border into Alpha Central, we had to stop the chase.'

'So, Farrell's escaped from prison. And he got help from Kane,' Tanner said in shock.

Hearing Farrell's name stabbed right into Jade. To the pit of her stomach. Knowing his threat and dangers, Jade knew she was driven to hunt him down at the first opportunity.

'Any lead as to why they'd help get Farrell out,' Jade asked.

'Rumours. Sketchy at best,' replied Louis. 'Word is that Farrell was able to sell drugs on the markets in Kane's territory. Kane knew he was mad, but worth the risk to do business with. All for the sake of profit.'

'What kind of business?' Jade asked.

'He paid Farrell to devise a brand new drug based on one called Benzodiazepine.'

'What?'

'Medical reports have it down as being a z listed drug. It's used as a sedative to calm those who are abnormally hyper. Or, in extreme cases, those seen as crazy or mad.'

'Well?' Jade asked.

'It's a drug that should only be taken by those it is prescribed to. The effects on the average person could lead to damaged side effects.'

'Like what?'

'Hypnotic overdose, brain damage. But if someone's given too strong a dose of the drug, the effect is a lethal seizure.'

'You think that's what he's planning?' Jade asked with sincere concern.

'Possibly. We can't rule anything out. Julius has put all police units on standby alert. All we can do is wait for his next strike. That's if there's meant to be one.'

'I know what he's capable of, Louis.'

'I know Jade. But if Farrell's made a deal with Kane, I suggest you both stay alert and vigilant. Kane's a powerful man. Enough to take over control of the whole city. If Kane is in league with him, that makes Farrell more dangerous than ever.'

Suddenly, Jade's instincts took over her thinking. She quickly took out her mobile phone and made a call. She turned her back to both Tanner and Louis.

Louis turned to speak back to Tanner.

'I must be getting back now, Frank.'

Tanner stood up from his chair and shook Louis' hand. 'Thank you, Louis. Thanks for all you could tell us.'

As Louis turned to leave, he could hear Jade in conversation on her phone. He gave her one last look, but she did not catch eye of his gesture. Her attention was elsewhere. Louis walked out of the office, shutting the door behind him.

Tanner stood listening on to what Jade was saying.

'That's good. Sean's okay, then? Great. It's fine. You stay with him at all times. OK, I'll see you later, Sarah. Take care. Bye.'

Jade ended the call. Breathing a huge sigh of relief. 'Who's

Sarah?' Tanner asked.

'Sean's nanny.'

'I'm sure he'll be fine.'

'Frank, how can things be fine knowing Farrell is out there?'

'Don't let your emotions control you over your thoughts, Jade. Just concentrate on your next case.'

'What case? I haven't been given one.'

'You have now. He's been waiting for you in your office. Jade, be careful. This case is really sensitive.'

'Don't worry. It's my job. I'll hold back from making it sensitive.'

Just then, Jade approached the side door on the adjacent wall leading into her office. Opening it and entering her office, she left Tanner to sit back down at his desk to look over his files and his own cases he had to deal with.

Chapter 12

Jade's office looked similar in style to Tanner's but was barer, tidier, and precise. No sight of files scattered over cupboards and tables. Jade kept a tight ship for making her office look professional and efficient. Jade noticed a man already sitting down facing towards her desk.

Jade approached the man to shake his hand. 'Hello, sir. I'm Private Detective Jade Hall.'

The man did not move. He continued looking ahead towards her desk. Nor did he make an effort to shake her hand. Instead, he gestured for Jade to sit down behind her desk. Jade felt slightly annoyed at the cold response the man had given her. But staying in her professional mode, Jade walked and sat in her chair. As she walked over, she got her first glimpse of the man clearly.

A man in his fifties, wearing a black hat, showing his age the years had taken on him. Dressed in a dark suit but not well dressed, he held onto his coat, letting it rest on his lap.

With Jade sat, she was trying to figure this man out. She sat quietly for a few seconds. Staring right into the man's eyes.

'So, what can I do for you?' Jade asked.

The man leant over the desk to hand Jade a photo. It was a photo of a boy. As Jade looked closely at it, the man took out a file that was hidden under his coat on his lap. Placing the file on Jade's desk. Looking at the photo of the boy, Jade looked up at the man to ask a question.

'Is the boy missing?' Jade asked.

The man said nothing and just simply nodded his head for yes.

'How long? Recently? Yesterday?'

The man again nodded his head for yes.

'Does he have a name?'

The man leant on the desk. He opened the file. He took out another photo. A school photo of the child with the name Jamie typed under the photo.

Jade wanted to know more. Curious to know more about this man in her office. 'Who are you? Who am I working for?'

Again, the man said nothing. He simply placed his finger up to his lips.

Can he not speak, Jade thought? *Is he used to not speaking? Has he been told not to speak? I suppose it doesn't matter. What matters is this child and returning the boy to his family.*

'OK,' Jade said. 'I'll find your boy for you. I'll find Jamie. I promise.'

*

Day had now become night. Jade remained sat at her desk. Ploughing through all the papers, documents, files that had all piled up from the information she had found in the past few hours. All on the disappearance of this boy, Jamie.

Detailing his birth, his respectable parents, upbringing, school, home address, etc. After reading all the personal details, Jade now was reading the transcripts of conversations made at police headquarters.

After reading them, she now had the time and place he was last seen in. Alpha Park playground.

Chapter 13

The next day, Jade was by herself. Walking down a path leading to the playground situated near one of the main entrances to Alpha Park. The largest park in the city.

The playground was typical of any you would find anywhere. Swings, roundabout, several metal benches scattered around. The playground was empty. Jade was all-alone. No other children or parents around. The park was peaceful and quiet.

Walking around the playground, Jade looked in all directions. The entrance to the park, the path by the side of the playground leading into the park, the wide-open space at the far end of the playground leading onto fields and grass.

Jade remembered looking at the files reading Jamie was last seen specifically sitting on the roundabout. She turned to look at the roundabout. Approaching it, she immediately lowered down so that her eye line was in parallel height with the top of the roundabout. On the opposite side to her nearest the park, were several benches. As she stood up, she sat on the roundabout. Roughly where Jamie would have been sitting. Where she was sat, she had her back to the benches and thereby, the main park area.

She tried to imagine being Jamie. Letting her eye-catching sight of large green bushes taller than her placed at the end of the playground nearest the trees and entrance to the park. Jade was curious to know more. Her instincts told her to look in the bushes.

She stood up from the roundabout and made her way

towards the tall green bushes.

In the bushes, she looked down to see a lot of grass on the surface. Rising up to knee level.

Virtually everywhere.

So, these bushes are not frequented in often, Jade thought. *If they were, the shoes would've rubbed away the grass and given way to a base of soil earth. Typically happens over grassy land that people frequent over regularly. So, a good spot to kidnap someone possibly? As no one comes into these bushes, no one is to suspect there would be someone in them. Clues, I need clues. Was the kidnapper in these bushes?*

Jade knelt down and started rummaging her fingers through the tall grass. Rooting around in the soil and earth. Her eye caught sight of light from the ground shining up into her face. The reflection of sunlight caught some glass in the ground nearby. She could see a small glass bottle a few feet away, peering out from just under the tall grass.

Moving closer in on the bottle, she took out of her coat pocket a pair of surgical rubber gloves. Placing them on, she carefully picked up the bottle. Examining it, she noticed the label had been ripped and torn off. She could see a very small drop of clear liquid still remaining on the inside base of the bottle. Undoing the bottle top, she sniffed to smell inside the bottle for any possible smell the liquid might have. But she could not make out any smell.

Placing the bottle top back on, her eyes scanned the bottle for any signs of fingerprints. There were no clear marks or finger stains on it. *The kidnapper must've worn gloves,* Jade thought.

As there was no more evidence Jade could see with the naked eye, she took out of her pocket a large clear sealant bag. Placing the bottle in the bag, she sealed it tight and placed the bag back in her coat pocket.

Taking her rubber gloves off, she turned her attention back towards the playground. Looking towards it, she could see a small opening from inside the bushes.

Moving closer towards the opening, she could see the opening gave her a near-clear view of the roundabout in the playground. As she began to walk forward out of the bushes, into the clear and into the playground, her eye got attracted to a large pole placed at the other end of the playground.

Looking up, at the top of the pole, was placed a C.C.T.V camera looking down on all of the playgrounds. Jade had a hunch. She had some more evidence to investigate.

Having made her way to the main park office block, Jade was now observing the C.C.T.V footage recorded the day Jamie disappeared.

She had taken out a note from her pocket. Scribbled on it was the time Jamie was last seen. Jade was fast-forwarding the footage to roughly a minute or so before Jamie was last seen.

Observing the footage, Jade watched Jamie sat alone on the still roundabout. She could see some adults sat down on the park benches in conversation. Presumably, relatives of Jamie not giving full attention as to what Jamie was doing. Jamie turned and looked at the bushes. Stepping off the roundabout, he walked towards the bushes. Suddenly, he was pulled from within by someone. After a minute, Jade noticed a masked man leave the bushes carrying a heavy sports bag. Then she sees him leave the park by the nearby park entrance gate.

Pressing pause, Jade stared at the masked kidnapper. She rewound the tape back to the moment he stepped out from the bushes.

Jade was intent on finding him. Her memories and her past

were stirring within her. Her emotions were beginning to drive her cause. Jade knew in her heart who that man was. All she needed now was the evidence to prove her point and to find Jamie alive.

Chapter 14

Later that day, Jade was now at the Police Headquarters forensics lab. Being helped by Louis Walker as a favour, several scientists were busy at work studying the liquid substance Jade discovered in the park.

Both she and Louis observed the tests being made from a distance. Standing in the far corner of the lab, Jade could not take her eyes off the tests. Louis, meanwhile, kept turning his head frequently towards her. Both had stood silent for a few minutes now. Louis was now starting to feel edgy and felt the need to speak first, break the ice and feel more comfortable.

'What do you hope to find?'

'Just that. Hope. For his family,' replied Jade.

'Noble. In the times we live in, it's hard to find hope anywhere. But it doesn't mean we should stop trying.'

Jade admired how Louis would always look at the glass half full. The feeling made her smile. She finally turned and gave attention to Louis. By doing this, she was expressing how appreciative she was of Louis' support and efforts in helping in her investigation.

'Thanks for helping me use this place,' Jade said.

'Anytime you need anything, Jade, all you have to do is ask.'

Suddenly, it dawned on Louis. He realised this was the first time he had been with Jade away from Tanner. He was curious to know more about the person she was. Tanner had already told him the facts of her past. But now, he was curious to know more about Jade, the person. And wanting to know how she coped with those dark memories.

'Jade, do you think back to the night your parents died?'

'I imagine it. Always,' replied Jade. 'I was a baby. I was there when they were murdered.'

'Is that why you became a private detective? To stop it happening to others?'

'Yes. I can help others. But after all I do, it'll never make me feel satisfied.'

'How do you mean?'

'I can never go back and be a detective on that night years ago. And help a little baby girl by stopping a killer take away her parents from her. That's the life she should've had. I should've had. That one night fuels me. The one case I can't solve. Because my parents' killer isn't here for me to catch, they never found him. I don't even know who it was. But if they're ever came a day when I could see him, I would pull the trigger and blow his brains out. And I'd do it with no regrets.'

Just then, a doctor approached both of them.

'We've analysed it. It's confirmed. It's the Z-listed drug. Benzodiazepine,' the doctor said.

With that knowledge, Jade wasted no time. Now she had the facts. She knew it was Farrell she was looking for. She quickly left the lab, followed by Louis. He knew how to help Jade find him and where to start looking.

*

Louis drove his car up to one of the old hospitals, now derelict. An old hospital called Alpha West General Hospital.

With Jade in the front passenger seat, Louis parked his car

77

across the street from the old A&E entrance. Turning off the engine, he pointed at the building. Giving Jade all the information he knew. 'When the hospital trust merged with Alpha Central Trust, they moved the hospital to a new site. Leaving this one empty and left to rot. A good place for Farrell to take advantage of the facilities no longer needed here.'

'It's the type of place Farrell would come to. All he needed was one of the labs.'

Just then, Jade undid her seat belt.

'Where you going?' Louis asked.

'I'm going to see if he's in there,' replied Jade.

'That big place? You can't go in alone, Jade.'

'I won't be.'

Jade got out her gun and started loading the empty barrels with bullets. She then told Louis what to do.

'Louis, call for backup. You stay here. If you hear gunshots, you'll know then I've got him.'

Jade gave Louis one last look before stepping out of the car and making her way towards the A&E entrance.

Watching her go, Louis got out his radio and started communicating back to police headquarters. 'Main Police Unit, I need full back up at the site formerly known as Alpha West General Hospital. A.S.A.P. Over.'

Chapter 15

Jade got her first view of the old reception area of the A&E department. Seeing empty metal chairs, the area deserted with files scattered along the floor, sheets of paper moving along the floor. Caught in the wind from the draught of air coming from the entrance doorway that Jade opened.

Blowing and moving about. Disturbing the faint traces of dust that cover the entire reception area.

Jade's long black coat caught the wind, too. Yet the wind blew towards her from inside the hospital. Draughts of wind from other open parts of the hospital blew in Jade's direction. Causing a slight cold chill in the air. She started moving down one of the long corridors. Holding her gun tight in hand. She heard silence. No sounds other than the rustling of papers caught up in the draught. The wind caused the sound of a breeze in her ears.

On a wall nearby, she saw an old map of the hospital. Looking for chemist shops and labs, she now had an idea of how to get to them. She started her cautious journey deeper into the heart of the old hospital.

*

Walking slowly and patiently down a long corridor, she could hear her footsteps from her heel boots echo down the long, empty, messy corridor. She remained mentally sharp and focused throughout her walk. She passed several windows. The Sun shone through them down onto the corridor floor. With the Sun breaking out, Jade looked out of the window to see some lovely greenery and trees she could see nearby. Relaxing very briefly at the beautiful sight of nature that she saw.

Suddenly, a faint echo sounded in the distance. Making Jade be alert once again. She stood still.

Staring ahead down the long, empty corridor. She could not make out what the echo sounded like. She slowed her breathing. Making it be more silent. She could feel a tension in the air. She stood as still as a mannequin so as she was able to be as sharp with her hearing as she could be.

But the echo had faded. She could not hear any more sounds up ahead. Jade cautiously began walking again ahead of her. Her footsteps again echoed down the long corridor.

*

Further along, Jade reached one of the main chemist labs. The door was closed. She placed her ear on the door. She heard nothing inside. With her free hand, she placed her hand gently on the door handle, turned it and slowly walked in.

Inside, the chemist was made up of desks, tables, and scattered chairs. Looking as deserted, scrappy, and messy as the rest of the hospital. Again, files and papers were scattered all over the floor.

The chemist expanded left and right of Jade. On the opposite wall where Jade stood was a long row of windows. Letting the Sunshine into the vast chemist.

Looking to her right, at the far end, Jade noticed it looked different to the mess the rest of the chemist looked like.

Approaching it, she saw it looked tidier and cleaner. Looking like the area had been made up like a small lab. With medicines, bottles, test tubes, Bunsen burners scattered among nearby desks and work benches. With a standing blackboard placed by the far wall, it reminded Jade more of a high school science lab.

Walking towards the blackboard, Jade started reading all the chemical formulas scribbled all over.

There was hardly anywhere left on the blackboard to scribble anything else down. Formulas of all different lengths and sizes took dominance over the entire area. Jade knew she was onto something.

I feel I'm getting closer to you, Farrell, Jade thought.

Then, looking at the edge of the blackboard, she noticed a piece of paper was flapping in the wind. It was stuck on the other side of the blackboard stand. Walking to look the other side, she noticed the paper was actually a photo. And it was the first of many photos. Roughly two dozen. Stuck with tape to the back of the stand. She looked at each one of the photos. Noticing they were photos all of children. Photos of them playing, being with friends or family, at home or at school. But she noticed a pattern. The photos each focused in on one child specifically. Ignoring other children and emphasising one particular child in each photo.

And then she saw him. Jade saw Jamie, the lost boy, in one of the photos. Recognising him instantly, Jade now knew she was onto something.

Having seen all there was to see, Jade went to leave the lab. Looking back towards the doorway entrance, she noticed a familiar figure standing there on the threshold. He looked older but still with the same venomous look in his crazed eyes.

Farrell, pointing a gun right at Jade with a maniacal smile, started shooting ferociously in her direction. Jade took her chance and ducked down for cover behind some tables and chairs.

Quickly, Jade scanned her body. Moving her hand over her body to see if she had been shot without her knowing. With no blood on her hand, Jade now knew the bullets had not hit her.

Farrell continued shooting towards the table Jade hid behind. Jade, with gun in hand, was ready to hit back. Waiting for her moment.

In his gun, Farrell had ran out of bullets. This was now her chance. She rose up and stood up straight. Aiming her gun at Farrell in the doorway.

She fired twice. Hitting him in his shoulder and right arm. The gunshots pushed Farrell back out into the corridor. With Farrell not in the doorway, the door swung shut.

Jade quickly ran towards the chemist's door. Swinging the door open, she pointed her gun out into the corridor.

But Farrell was nowhere to be seen. Jade stood still. She could hear the echo of running footsteps.

But she could not make out which direction they were coming from.

Jade then looked down to the floor. She saw a blood trail from Farrell's wounds leading off down the corridor to the right.

Jade ran down, following the trail. Looking back and forth between the blood trail on the ground and up ahead of her. The trail led her to a staircase. The trail started going up.

Hearing Farrell's fast footsteps echoing more clearly from the staircase up above, Jade looked up the spiral. Seeing Farrell's hand on the handle three or four floors above.

Jade started sprinting up the staircase. Determined to catch him and not let him get away.

Reaching the fourth floor, the trail turned right, leaving the staircase, and going underneath a nearby closed door. Jade readied herself. Standing in front of the door, pointing her gun ahead.

She slammed her foot hard on the door. Forcing it open, she took a few steps in.

*

Jade had walked into a vast old hospital ward. Spread long and far down with a high ceiling. The area where hospital beds were once placed had been replaced by large wooden crate boxes that were taller than Jade. Scattered all over the ward, the area now looked more like a warehouse. The large windows were now smashed in. No glass left in them at all. The only things left were the blinds flapping hard and fast from the wind coming through the open windows.

Up ahead, Jade noticed no symmetry or clear path to walk between the large crates. The crates had now made the ward become a large maze to walk through. But it was too late to go back now. Now she knew she was this close to getting Farrell.

But now she saw her problem. Her disadvantage. A few paces in front of her, she saw the blood trail stop clearly between the crates. *He's bandaged the wound,* thought Jade. She now had no idea where Farrell could be. And he would be the one who knew this maze better than Jade.

Hearing no footsteps, Jade walked on with caution. Her heart rate was starting to go faster. Her mouth becoming dryer. She carefully looked around the corner of the crates in front of her. Still, there was no sight or sound of Farrell.

Just then, bullets shot towards her from a distance away up ahead. Jade fell to the floor. Moving and hiding behind a couple of crates. She knew Farrell had reloaded his gun and most likely, he was now standing nearer to where he stocked the rest of his supplies. As the shooting stopped, Jade heard the sound of his voice. A voice sounding, in the echo, like a distant memory had returned.

'So princess, you want to play? Let's play bitch,' Farrell shouted out.

He started shooting again in Jade's direction. She was safe and covered by the crates. Once he stopped shooting, he shouted out again.

'I knew it was only a matter of time before you came here. But I needed a good chemist. I love being a chemist. So, you know what, princess? I think we should now have that party we should've had all those years ago.'

Again, Farrell shot in Jade's direction. Then he stopped after a few seconds.

'Aren't you going to say hello, princess?'

Just then, Jade took her chance. Looking around the corner of the crates and shooting back in Farrell's direction. Then she moved back to have cover behind the crates. Giving her time to get out bullets from her pocket and reload the barrel of her gun.

'That's the spirit,' Farrell shouted out.

Suddenly, Jade turned away from the edge of the crate and looked towards the nearby wall. She had a path to it. With cover from the crates stopping her being shot at, she started moving slowly towards the wall. Meanwhile, Farrell continued shouting across the vast space.

'I knew the drugs would lead to this. All I want is the kids to get high and have a good time. It's time to loosen up and have a lot more highs. Where are you, girl? Have you gone shy on me?'

Jade reached the wall without being seen. She looked down

the long stretch of the wall towards the far end. She saw she had space to move further down deeper into the ward. She could hear Farrell's footsteps. She knew he was close.

Nearby, Jade saw a large plank of wood on the ground. She slowly lowered down to the floor and picked it up. She threw it towards a distance far away. Hoping to fool Farrell into thinking that was where she was. Jade saw where it landed. She had set the trap for Farrell to follow the sound and come into clear view. She waited. And waited. Hearing his footsteps.

Then, she felt the warm metal of a gun barrel touching the side of her neck. Now she knew she was in trouble.

'Hello, princess. You didn't fool me with that trick with the plank. Drop the gun,' Farrell demanded.

Jade let her gun drop. Farrell moved to stand behind Jade. Moving in to be aroused at the smell of her hair and body fragrance. Taking it all in, in a perverted sexual way.

'It's a shame you're still not a little girl for me,' Farrell said. 'But it's time we have our special moment together. The one we should've had last time.'

Still holding the gun to her neck, with his other hand, Farrell took out a needle and syringe from his pocket. Biting off the needle cover, he squeezed down on the syringe, letting the chemical liquid shoot out. Farrell was ready to inject Jade with it.

'To make up for last time,' Farrell said whilst whispering in Jade's ear, 'I've doubled up the dosage just for you princess. Because you're a good girl. You're very special to me.'

'You forgot something, Farrell,' Jade said quietly.

'What's that baby girl?' Farrell asked.

'You forgot to cover all your bases,' replied Jade, leaving Farrell puzzled at what she meant.

As Jade knew Farrell held his gun in one hand and a syringe in the other, she took the chance to clench her fist so tight she spun 180 degrees around to face Farrell. Punching him painfully hard in his genitals with passion. Her fist was so strong it felt like a large rock had hit Farrell in the most sacred part of his body.

Farrell screamed out loud from the pain. Pushing him back against the wall. With no time for Farrell to think properly, Jade kicked Farrell's gun out of his hand. Punching him hard in the face several times. Making him go faint and dazed. She broke his jaw and nose. Blood poured down from both of them.

Now weakened, Farrell could not stop Jade taking the syringe out of his hand. Without a second thought, Jade inserted the needle into Farrell's neck. Pressing down on the syringe until there was no chemical liquid left in it. It was now all inside Farrell's body.

Jade stepped back, letting the drug do its business. She picked up her gun off the floor. Then pointed it right at Farrell's head.

As the drug took effect, Farrell lost balance and started sliding slowly down the wall. He started to smile, frothing at the mouth, with his eyes becoming bloodshot red. He was now completely drugged up.

'Wow. What a massive feeling this is, princess,' Farrell said with his words starting to slur.

Slowly, the overdose was beginning to take effect. Farrell stopped moving less and less. His face turned pale white. Bloody tears started coming out of his eyes. His breathing was becoming slower.

Then he sat still. Farrell was dead.

Jade, looking down at Farrell's corpse, lowered her gun. Then she quietly spoke. 'I'm nobody's princess. Rot in hell. You sick freak.'

After a few seconds, not wanting to dwell any more time on Farrell than she had to, Jade walked away at a fast pace.

Why did you come to this floor, Farrell? Jade thought. *Are you hiding Jamie near here?*

Jade made her way through the maze of crates. Moving towards the far end of the hospital ward.

At the end was a closed door. Banging it open, she pointed her gun forward. Beyond the door was a corridor of closed doors. Lowering her gun, she stepped up to each door left and right of her.

Opening each door and shouting into each room. 'Jamie! Jamie!'

With all the rooms empty, Jade made her way down the long corridor. Finally, reaching the last door that was neither left nor right of her but was directly in front of her. Jade tried to open the door. It was locked. She took a few steps back and started running up towards the door and slamming it wide open.

Jade looked inside the room. Standing still, she could see a child's body lying motionless on the floor. She saw a syringe hanging out of the child's right arm. Jade recognised the child and knew who it was. She saw him in the same condition she saw Farrell in the last few seconds of his life.

'No. No,' Jade quietly said.
It was too late. Jamie, the lost child, had been found dead.

Chapter 16

The days past by with Jade not being able to shake off her failure from her mind. She felt it only right to attend Jamie's funeral several days later. Grey clouds covered the sky above. Slight amounts of rain were trickling down on this the darkest of emotional days.

Although she wanted to be there, Jade felt it inappropriate to be close to the family for the service.

She felt it was more respectful to be there and yet keep her distance.

And so, in Southern Cemetery, as Jamie's family and friends watched the service, seeing Jamie's coffin being moved and lowered into his grave, Jade stood back about a hundred yards away under a large tree.

Several members of the family noticed Jade nearby but did not respond to her being there.

Catching a glimpse, they turned their attention back to the coffin.

Behind Jade, she heard footsteps approach her. She did not turn to see who it was. But she had a good idea who it would be.

It was Tanner. Now, he stood side by side with her. Both looking on at Jamie's funeral service. Jade was the first to speak.

'I now know why you came to my friend's funeral all those years ago. It was guilt. Failing to right the wrong. Doing that, showing your face at the funeral was the noble gesture to those you should answer to. I failed Frank.'

'There was nothing more you could've done,' Tanner replied.

'Yes, there was,' Jade passionately said. 'If I was quicker, sharper, faster with my thoughts, I could've saved him.'

'Jade, you gave his family justice. They told me. They appreciated what you did. You got Farrell. The one who took Jamie from them.'

'It's not enough. This funeral today shows that's never enough. This should not be happening. He should be home with his family. Not having them bury him.'

Jade could not take being there any more. She started walking away. Leaving Tanner and the funeral service.

'Jade,' Tanner shouted.

She stopped and looked back at Tanner. Hearing what he had to say.

'I told you this case would be sensitive. Be professional. Don't be fuelled by emotions. Draw a line in the sand and move on.'

'You know what, Frank?' Jade replied, 'Maybe that's the difference between me and you. You can draw a line and move on. I can't.'

Jade had said enough. She continued walking to leave the cemetery. Leaving Tanner to stay watching over the rest of Jamie's funeral service.

*

Sometime later, Jade was slowly walking her way back towards the private detective offices on Dale Street. She had reached nearby and was standing by the Alpha City Gardens in the city centre. Jade's thoughts still pondered on Jamie and the funeral service earlier in the day. Still dwelling on the events that led to the unfortunate loss of life of the young child.

Suddenly, she became distracted by her mobile phone ringing constantly. The ringing made her become more alert and awake from her thoughts. Answering the call from a withheld number, she placed the mobile phone up to her ear.

'Hello?'

Jade heard a deep masculine voice speaking to her from the other end.

'Killing Farrell doesn't stop anything. He was the tip of the iceberg, Jade Hall.'

She did not recognise the voice, but felt concerned of his intentions by how he was speaking to her in a threatening way.

'Who is this?' Jade asked.

The deep male voice replied, 'You failed to save a child. Try saving your own.'

He hung up. Jade lowered the phone down. *Kane wants to get his own back on me,* Jade thought. *Oh my God. Sean.*

Jade started running faster than she ever had before. She had to get to her son Sean. Making sure he was safe.

*

The flat Sean was in was peaceful and happy. Jade and Sean lived in a flat within the city centre called the Hacienda Apartments. Formally, the site of the aforementioned club.

Sean was in the living room. On the floor, playing with his toys whilst watching a children's programme on TV.

Sarah, Sean's nanny, was sat on the settee, overlooking what Sean was doing and making sure he was okay. She, too, was all smiles and happy like Sean.

The two of them were alone. No one else was present in the flat.

*

Jade frantically ran fast. Making her way down Portland Street, then cutting across through Chorlton Street and turning again. Running down the long stretch of Canal Street. A shortcut route to get to the Hacienda apartments faster. Breathing steadily, she ran like an athlete.

Reaching the Palace Theatre, she had come to the main road of Oxford Road. Wanting to cross quickly, the road was filled with cars, vans and buses moving fast in either direction.

Taking her chance, she ran in front of all the vehicles. Drivers are beeping their horns at her. Stopping their vehicles. Making sure they did not crash into her or run her over. Still, she made it across the road.

On the other side of the road was Whitworth Street West. A long stretch of street that housed at the end of the stretch the Hacienda Apartments.

Running down the street, passing the Ritz concert hall, Jade made a call to the apartment. Placing the phone up to her ear, she could hear the phone starting to ring.

*

Hearing the phone ringing, Sarah stood up and left the living room. Walking into the hallway, she picked up the main phone for the flat and answered the call.

'Hello?'

*

'Sarah,' Jade shouted as she ran. 'Get Sean and you out of the flat now.'

As the street bended to the right, Jade saw round the edge of the corner the entrance to the apartments. She was almost there.

'Jade, are you okay? What's wrong?' Sarah asked worryingly.

*

Sarah became quickly concerned. She turned and walked back into the living room. Her instincts kicked in to go to Sean and make sure he was fine.

Looking down at the smiling, playful Sean, Sarah started to panic and feel afraid. 'Jade? Where are you?' Sarah asked.

Little did Sarah know that by answering the phone, it had triggered the bomb. Hidden underneath the table, the receiver was placed upon. It was counting down.

four…three…two…one

*

BANG!

Reaching the entrance, Jade looked up. The flames exploded out of her flat windows. Glass shattering and falling to the ground. Jade covered her head. Several small pieces of glass scratched her face. Moving her hands from her face, Jade looked up in shock. Standing still. Several other people near her in the street looked up, too, in shock.

'SEAN! NO! SEAN!'

Jade screamed out louder than she ever had before. She started trying to open the door of the main entrance. Her instincts as a parent took over. She wanted to get up there and try to save her son. But the sight of the flames was telling their own story.

Several people nearby held Jade back for her own protection from the flames. Pushing her further and further back from the blaze that was now large and alight in the apartment block.

Tears endlessly streamed down Jade's face. Her eyes were full of emotion. Becoming bloodshot red within seconds. She continued to scream as she cried.

'MY BABY! MY BABY! THEY KILLED HIM! THEY KILLED HIM!'

Jade repeated the words over and over again. All the while looking up at the fire, blaze and smoke coming out of the flat several floors up.

Her face was now wet from tears, screaming out Sean's name continuously. Her pain and loss now enveloping her whole body and emotions.

Never taking her eyes off the flames, she collapsed and fell down to her knees on the floor.

Constantly repeating her son's name.

'SEAN! SEAN! SEAN!'

*

Nearby, on a bridge overlooking the street and apartments, was the tram stop for Deansgate-Castlefield. Standing alone on the platform was a well-suited black man observing the flames from the flat explosion. He stood alone. Seeing that everything went as planned, he now looked down on the helpless Jade.

The suited man made a call on his phone. He stood waiting for an answer. He spoke with the natural, deep, masculine voice he spoke to Jade with only minutes earlier.

'It's done,' the suited man said. Then he hung up the phone.

As this was the man called Parker, a professional bomb expert who planted the bomb, he turned and started to leave the platform. Leaving the scene of his expertise. Leaving Jade to soak up her loss from the explosion Parker had put together.

Chapter 17

Day had now turned to night. Jade sat alone on a metal bench in a hospital corridor at the Alpha Children's Hospital. Doctors and nurses passed by her all busy at work. The corridor stretched far and long down each end on either side of her.

Her tears had now dried up. Jade was now exhausted and drained from the horrific event she had witnessed. She felt her heart's pain now more than ever. She paid no attention to anyone or anything that was around her. In her mind's eye, all she saw was the smiling face of Sean. The only thing that meant everything to her. But her pain was growing as the reality was sinking in. Telling her the painful fact that she would never see him smile ever again. And worse, never saying the word that meant so much to both of them.

Mummy.

'Miss Hall.'

A nurse was standing beside Jade. Hearing her name called made Jade wake up from her thoughts.

She looked up at the nurse. Jade's face looked drained, with barely any expression on it. 'Miss Hall, would you like to see him one last time?' the nurse asked her.

Jade said nothing but slowly started nodding her head yes. The nurse offered her hand to Jade. Gently helping her rise up from her chair. Jade followed the nurse towards a closed door for a private room.

Just then, far away at one end of the corridor, Tanner had

found his way onto the correct ward.

Having heard the tragic news earlier on, he had rushed quickly to the hospital so he could be here for Jade.

With so much happening, with many doctors, nurses and patients filling up the space in the corridors, Tanner caught a glimpse of Jade being shown into a private room. He saw her walk in, then seeing the nurse close the door and then walking away leaving Jade by herself in the private room.

Tanner walked up to the closed door. Staring at it, he felt ready to walk in.

Then suddenly, a hesitant emotion came over him. *Is this the right thing?* he thought. This is about Sean. Her last moment with him.

Tanner suddenly felt that this was the wrong time. He started to feel like she might not want to see him right now. Knowing Jade well, he thought that her anger would be so strong that she might take out her anger for her loss on him.

Tanner knew better that he did not want to see that side of her. He had seen that in her as a child.

What anger would she give out now she was a woman and a mother?

He stepped back from the closed door. Then he started walking away and leaving the ward.

Feeling torn between wanting to help her and knowing she would not want help right now. He was also feeling the regret of not knowing what the best choice was to make at that important moment. Tanner walked away, torn, and ashamed.

*

Jade stood still within the small private room. It was cold and

96

nearly dark. A white spotlight from the ceiling shone down on the hospital bed placed in the centre of the room.

A white sheet completely covered the small body lying on top of the bed. Jade remained still.

The room was completely silent.

She stared forward at the bed and the white sheet. Standing by the closed door, she was almost afraid to move forward towards the bed. Knowing with each step she took, the pain she felt in her heart as a mother would grow stronger and more painful.

But she knew she had to take those steps. She knew she had to see the truth for what it was. She wanted to see her son again.

She took one step. Then two. Then three. Her eyes filled with tears the nearer she got to the bed. Reaching it, she felt less like a woman but more that of a mother. Slowly, she reached forward.

Gently grasping the white sheet and moving it down the bed.

The sight of her dead son's face felt like an instant stab in her heart and soul.

The main purpose of her life, her son Sean, was gone. The purpose of being a mother, nurturing her son, watching him grow, becoming a man, falling in love, having a family of his own. All gone. Forever.

His face was all burnt as black as coal. His eyes were closed. Parts of the flesh on his burnt body were as red as flesh meat.

Jade painfully thought, *A parent should never have to lose their child.* Knowing their child is now dead.

She looked down at his body. Tears now streaming down her face. She spoke out very quietly.

Choked up at the emotion she now felt so deeply. 'Look at the mess of my little boy.'

Jade slowly lowered her hand onto his black and burnt

chest. Not wanting to press too hard on it.

Jade, illogically, thought that pressing her hand harder down on his body would hurt him even more.

But then, knowing he would not move nor react, she finally gave a firm grip of her hand on his chest. Still hoping to feel the beat of his heart. And yet she felt nothing.

'I'm so sorry, Sean,' Jade said. 'Please forgive me.'

The room remained silent. Jade's tears began to stop. Her mother instincts were beginning to surface. Overcoming the pain she felt.

She lowered down her head. Gently kissing his burnt forehead. Stroking his head with her hand, she quietly whispered in his ear for the very last time.

'Goodnight, my baby. Sweet dreams, my angel.'

Chapter 18

With her flat now destroyed, Jade made home for the night back at her office on Dale Street.

Taking off her coat and throwing it across her desk, she sat down, collapsing in her desk chair. Leaning her head so far back, she was looking up at the ceiling.

Leaving the lights switched off in her dark office, the street lamp post outside shone up the ceiling nearer the window and her desk. Staring blankly up at the ceiling, Jade felt hopeless and empty at that moment. Feeling she now had no purpose. The world for her now felt very hollow.

Jade felt exhausted to the point of feeling calm. Hearing the faint city sounds outside the window, the office remained peaceful and silent.

Suddenly, Jade heard a rustle of noise over by her closed office door. An envelope had been slid in under the door.

Jade quickly stood up, grabbed her gun from out of her coat, ran quickly over to the door and opened it. She stepped out into the corridor to see who had placed the envelope at the base of her door. But Jade was surprised to see no one there. She could hear nothing. No movement or sound of footsteps.

Thinking quickly, Jade ran back into her office towards the window. Looking down onto the street, Jade saw that no one had left the building. Whoever had delivered the envelope had made sure not to stay and to get away quickly without being seen by anyone, even by Jade.

Why would they do that? Jade thought. *What was it they wanted me to know?*

Curious to know more, Jade knew the only answer she was going to get would be in the envelope.

She walked over and picked up the envelope off the floor. It was very light in weight. Opening it, she took out a letter inside. Also, inside was a plastic white card that was blank with no description on it. Reading the letter, it was printed out. There was no way of knowing who had sent or delivered the envelope. It was an anonymous letter with some very important news. It read:

TIP OFF. YOU'LL FIND WHO KILLED YOUR SON AT THE NORTHERN POWERHOUSE FINANCE BUILDING, SPINNINGFIELDS. ROOM 304. THE WHITE CARD WILL GIVE YOU ACCESS TO THE BUILDING. GOOD LUCK.

With that, Jade's energy woke up. Her adrenaline started pumping faster. The anger in her began firing up inside her. Growing stronger with every second. Jade knew exactly what she was going to do.

*

Jade parked her car along a stretch of city centre road called Deansgate. It was now very late at night. The area was quiet and empty. No one else was around.

Looking out of the car, across the street was the Northern Powerhouse finance building. Formerly, the offices of a now liquidated national bank in Alpha City. The building was lit up, with each floor made up of glass walls. Covering from top to bottom. Spinningfields was the trendy upmarket business area of the city centre. If you had any money, this was the place to work.

The building looked quiet. The perfect time for Jade to find out more about whoever was behind the bomb that killed her son.

Stepping out of her car, Jade walked across the road. Making her way towards the secured locked main entrance. Getting out the white plastic card from her coat pocket, she placed the card on a small screen on the wall beside the main door. It was a contactless key. Making the glass main door open. Jade walked into the reception area. Instantly walking towards the lifts, pressing the button, and waiting for the lift to reach the ground floor.

*

Several minutes later, Jade was walking down a formal business corridor several floors above. At a steady pace, she looked at the numbers to each door she passed. Room 299. 300. 301. 302. 303. And then.

304.

Jade got out her gun. Holding it with a firm grip. Her heart was racing fast. *Was the murderer behind this door?* she thought. *I hope so,* she thought again.

Gently, she placed her hand on the door handle. Slowly making it turn, she opened the door.

Looking inside, the room was dark. It seemed there was no one in the room presently. Jade felt disappointed and frustrated.

However, Jade did not want to waste time. She saw the office was clean, formal, designed with trendy office chairs, table, desk, settee, art works placed all around the walls. Opposite where Jade stood was a fully glassed wall from ceiling to floor. Stretched wide, meeting the two side walls on either side of it. The glass

101

wall overlooked the city. The office desk and chair were placed in front of it.

Closing the door shut, Jade made her way over towards the desk. Opening the desk drawer, Jade saw nothing valuable to help her. All she found were formal stationery items. Nothing to identify who this office belonged to.

Turning away, Jade looked out of the glass wall window. Looking down, she could see the side street that ran alongside the building just off Deansgate. More importantly, she noticed a car being parked up on the street directly beneath her, right next to the building.

Observing, Jade saw a man wearing a formal business suit step out of the car, locked it, and then entered the building by the main entrance. Exactly the same way Jade had entered the building with the white plastic contactless key card. Jade knew there was a chance this was the man she was after.

Thinking quickly, Jade walked with a fast pace back towards the office door. Standing by the wall, the door would swing towards when opened. Jade calmly readied her gun. She stood waiting patiently. Wanting the door to the office to open from outside. With each second, her pulse rate got faster. She could nearly feel the heartbeat against her chest.

She could hear outside in the corridor the soft footsteps slowly getting louder in volume. She knew the man was in the corridor outside, literally just on the other side of the wall.

Jade turned and looked down at the door handle. She saw it move down. Watching it turn. Then the door opened.

The businessman switched on the main light to the office. Walking in, he swung around to close the door shut. As he did, he saw Jade pointing her gun at his head. Shocked to see her, the businessman had no time to think before Jade whacked her gun hard into his face. The force of the impact made the businessman fall down to the floor. He touched his head with his hand. Jade had made his forehead start to bleed. He was in shock. He looked up at Jade. Standing above him. Pointing her gun down right at his head.

'Who are you?' the bald, squeaky voice, thin, older white businessman said.

Just then, Jade turned her gun and shot the man in his right foot. He screamed out in pain instantly. The blood pouring out of the wound started soaking into the carpet.

Jade turned her gun back at the bald businessman's face. 'Who was it that rang me?' Jade asked violently.

'What?' the bald businessman said with a puzzled tone in his squeaky voice.

'It wasn't your voice on the phone to me this afternoon. I'll ask again. Who was it that rang me?' Jade spoke fiercely now.

'I don't know what you're talking about,' he said quickly.

'I want to know who it was who rang me minutes before my son was murdered. Tell me!' Jade shouted angrily. She lowered her gun so that it was now touching the temple on the side of the bald man's head.

'Please don't kill me. Please. Please. I'll tell you who it was,' the bald man insisted.

'You better tell me now. I swear.'

'It was Parker. It was his job. I helped him get the explosives and the equipment.'

'Where's Parker now?'

'He's at a meeting with a client. I don't know where.'

'Anything else?'

'That's all I know. I swear. Parker knows everything.'

In anger, Jade punched the bald man hard in the face. Picking him up off the floor, Jade threw him over the office desk. The bald man rolled over the desk. Falling off it onto the floor. Nearby, the large glass wall. Walking towards him, Jade ran up and kicked him hard in the stomach again and again. From the punch and hit of the gun on his face, the bald man's face started to swell and become bruised.

As Jade stopped kicking him, the bald man looked out of the window, directly down into the street below. He saw a black man in a suit get out of a car that had just parked up in the side street near where his own car was. The bald man recognised him. He suddenly got excited, thinking this was the hope that Jade would stop what she was doing to him. He desperately told Jade.

'That's him. Down there. That's Parker. That's him.'

Jade looked out of the window to see Parker. Now, knowing what he looked like, Jade was determined to meet him. But first, she still had one thing left to do.

Jade quickly grabbed hold and picked up the bald businessman off the floor. Making him stand up. She held a strong grip on him in one hand whilst holding and pointing her gun at his head with the other.

'Well,' Jade said, 'as I'm done with you, you'd better say hello to Parker down there.'

The bald man looked puzzled and confused. Then he saw Jade move her gun away from him, pointing it at the glass wall. She shot at the window three times, making it crack all of the glass. Only then, when Jade was looking back at him, did he know what she was going to do. Then, he became worried even more when he saw the anger deep in her eyes.

'No. Please. No,' he said with fear and panic. But it was too late.

Jade threw the bald man towards the cracked glass wall window. Throwing him out of the office.

Shattering the glass wall instantly.

Jade stood looking down out of the open wall. Watching the bald businessman fall further and further down to the ground. Watching, as she put it, the bald businessman saying hello to the man she was now after, Parker.

Chapter 19

BANG! CRASH! SMASH!

The bald businessman crashed down dead in the middle of his own car. Forcing the car roof to crush in on itself. The car alarm was sounding loud and endlessly.

Parker stood in shock from the explosion of noise. He stood back as thousands of small fragments of glass covered the smashed car and the area surrounding it.

After a few seconds, Parker approached the smashed car. He recognised the corpse of the bald businessman. Parker stood in amazement at the image he saw in front of him.

Looking up at the office block, he saw the opening of the smashed window where the bald man had fallen from. He noticed the light shining from the lit room. As well as noticing the figure of someone standing there looking down at him, it was unclear who it was. The light from the room obscured any clear distinction of who it could be.

All he saw was the silhouette of the long, dark-haired woman, the long black coat, and the gun in her hand. The draught of wind bursting into the smashed window opening caught her hair and coat. Blowing them everywhere. Yet it did not disturb her. She stood still. Looking down like a predator. Ready to catch her next prey. And Parker knew it was him she was ready to hunt for.

Parker took his chance. He began quickly running back towards his parked car across the street.

The female figure pointed her gun down at him. Aiming and shooting him hard in his left shoulder. Parker screamed out in pain. Falling down to the ground.

Looking ahead of him, Parker was still several feet away from his car. Suddenly, he saw a bullet missing him, hitting the ground nearby. He knew he could not stay here. Parker picked himself up off the floor. A third bullet shot into his right leg. He screamed out aloud again in pain. Not far from his car, he was able to collapse on the bonnet.

He held a grip of his wounded shoulder, looking up at the building and at the woman in the window opening. Suddenly, a thought crossed his mind.

It's Jade, he thought, *how did she find me?*

Just then, knowing the female figure was her, he saw her walk away from the window opening.

Moving deeper into the office until Parker could not see her. He knew where she was going. She was on her way out of the office and making her way back down to street level. The race was on. Parker had about a minute, maybe less, to get away from here.

Struggling, Parker, with all his strength, moved to the driver's seat door of his car. Parker got out his keys, unlocked the door and got in the driver's seat. All the while looking back and forth towards the building's main entrance reception area. Hoping not to see the lift door open and watch Jade step out.

The lobby remained empty as Parker attempted to switch on the ignition. As Parker got it on, just then, he saw the lift door open. And out stepped Jade with gun in hand.

Parker wasted no time. He put his foot down and sped fast down the street. Passing the building, he looked at his side rear view mirror. Seeing Jade run out into the middle of the road, pointing her gun at his car, she smashed the rear window of Parker's car with the bullets from her gunshots. But Parker aimed to not get disturbed by the gunshots. He continued to focus on the road up ahead and get away from the area as fast as he could.

But Parker had looked one last time in his side rear view mirror to see, back at the far end of the road, Jade running fast back towards her parked car. Seeing her get in and begin following him in pursuit. Parker was a marked man and he knew his time was short.

*

Jade, with one hand on the wheel, reloaded her gun full of new bullets with her free hand. She placed the gun in the passenger's seat beside her. Then she picked up her mobile phone off the dashboard. Making a call, she placed the phone up to her ear. Hearing the call ring out, her eyes stayed focused on the road and following Parker's car up ahead as she drove.

'Hello?' Tanner said at the other end of the line.

'It's me,' Jade said. 'I found the man who murdered Sean. I'm chasing him down. Follow the signal from my phone.'

Quickly, Jade hung up the phone, throwing it down on the seat next to her.

*

Meanwhile, Parker made a call of his own. Waiting for someone to answer at the other end. When they did, Parker spoke in a desperate tone with his deep, distinctive voice.

'It's Parker. I've been shot. Very bad. My partner Wilson's dead. I think it's that detective Jade after me. Help me out. Get me out of this situation now.'

Parker ended the call. Now, he gave his full attention back towards the nightly city main road he was driving fast down.

*

Across town, at the Alpha City Police Headquarters, Louis Walker was sat by his desk, quietly busy at work, looking over several police enquiries. As were the several dozen other officers present at this time of night.

Suddenly, Julius Carver stormed into the main office. Shouting loudly for everyone to hear and pay attention.

'Everybody shut up and listen. Just got a tip-off. Jade Hall has just murdered a man and is in pursuit of another. We must get Jade before anybody else gets killed. I need you all out there in pursuit. Now!'

Instantly, all the officers present stood up and started leaving the department and offices. As they did, Julius stopped Louis from leaving.

'Louis, you know Jade, don't you? You could be useful. Don't go with the rest. Follow me.'

'Yes, sir,' Louis replied. Both Julius and Louis left the department by a different exit than the other officers took. They were going to follow the pursuit by different means.

*

Parker's nerves started to grow. Feeling his brow beginning to sweat as he saw two car headlamps moving in closer towards the rear of his car. He knew whose car it belonged to. His heartbeat was increasing very quickly.

Looking in his rearview mirror, he could see Jade and the look of anger in her eyes. To Parker, the look was bordering on rage. Quickly, Jade moved into the next lane on Parker's right, speeding up fast to be in parallel with his car.

Parker put his foot down to increase speed, but Jade was matching him in that department. The two cars remained side by side each other in parallel.

Parker turned his head to see Jade in her car keeping one hand on the steering wheel. And holding her gun with her other hand. Pointing right at Parker's head. In a split second, Parker's heart rate raced up. Starting to make him panic more.

Just then, he looked back up ahead of him. Concentrating his focus back onto the road, he was speeding fast towards a wall directly in front of his car. The road was turning off left and right ahead of him. Jade had noticed the turn earlier than Parker. Causing her instantly to slow her car down.

The speed of his car made Parker know he was past the point of no return. Accelerating too fast, he desperately turned his car off for the left turn. The angle for turning was now too steep. He saw nothing ahead of him except a brick wall.

The right side of his car slammed hard against the wall. Jerking his body to the right causing a whiplash effect. The car scraped forward along the wall for several more feet until it came to a dead halt.

Parker, now dazed, sat still in his seat. His forehead, now cut, started bleeding trickles of blood down the side of his head.

He could hear his car engine still running. His sight was blurry from the cause of the crash. It was dark inside his car. Then, light slowly lit up his car. Helping him become more conscious again.

Waking up, he knew the light was coming from the

headlamps of Jade's car. He saw the lights pointing right at him. The car was still and not moving some twenty feet away. Now fully awake, Parker knew Jade was far from finished with him.

Jade's car sped fast into life. Driving directly towards Parker's car. He put his foot down. Speeding fast again down the road. His car, now damaged, still remained in good condition.

Jade continued her pursuit. Following Parker wherever he chose to go. Jade was silently happy Parker was still alive and conscious for her to pursue.

*

Above the Alpha City skyline, Julius was accompanied by Louis in a police helicopter. Scanning their observation over the whole city. Waiting for any reports to come in. Looking themselves for any trace of the two cars within the city centre. A trained pilot accompanied them in their search.

Louis observed a night vision monitor that spanned several hundred yards in all directions. He could not yet pick up any trace of a car chase nearby.

Julius, sitting beside him, took to observing outside the side of the helicopter window. Focusing more on any possible activity happening directly beneath them.

With the city lights lit up as far as the eye could see, the landscape looked similar to that of Los Angeles. Briefly admiring the city landscape view, Julius turned his attention back to Louis.

'Have you found them yet?' Julius asked.

'No sir. No sign of them,' replied Louis.

'Find them quick. We're running out of time.'

*

Back down on the city streets, Tanner drove his car fast down a city centre road. Continuing to track Jade's signal from her phone, it became a signal like a Satnav for him to reach Jade.

Knowing where she was, he knew he was still some distance away from her. It would still take him a good five or ten minutes to reach her. Provided the chase would come to a halt, Tanner was determined to reach Jade in time before it was too late.

*

With Parker still in front, Jade sped fast up to the rear of his car. Parker shook, reacting to the bump hitting his car. He remained steady with his hands on the wheel. Trying not to get distracted any more from Jade's attempts.

Jade did it again. Speeding fast again up to the rear of Parker's car. This time, with an even harder bump.

With more power in the second bump, Parker struggled to maintain control of his steering. Losing control, his car quickly moved left and right but still was going forward. Parker noticed Jade was getting ready to speed up and bump his car for a third time. He took his chance. Looking up ahead, he could see a possible turn-off into a multi-storey car park.

Desperately making a quick, sudden choice, he turned his car off the road, driving towards the car park entrance. Jade's car continued speeding fast past him down the road.

Before entering the car park, Parker took a quick look at Jade's car further on down the road.

Parker grew nervous as he saw Jade spin her car around one hundred and eighty degrees. Starting to make her way back down the road towards the car park entrance. Parker was now sober to think he was now in trouble. He knew his fate was about to catch up with him. His fate came in the name of Jade Hall.

Chapter 20

Driving up fast on each floor of the car park, Parker knew he was now trapped. Making sharp turns up to the next level, the screeches from his car tyres echoed loudly throughout the multi-storey car park.

Being late at night, the car park was empty. Nowhere for Parker to hide. Taking no chances, Parker drove further up and up. Reaching the last line of defence, he drove onto the top floor rooftop. Making his car come to a halt.

With his adrenaline wearing off, the pain from his gunshot wounds began to increase. Parker was now exhausted. His breathing became heavier. He now leaned his body against his car door. Slowly opening up the door, his body collapsed out of the car. Falling down onto the concrete.

It was beginning to rain. The water falling on Parker's face felt refreshing for a brief moment. He could hear nothing but the faint, distant sounds of nightlife. Cars are travelling down nearby roads and motorways. Resting his head on the floor, Parker was now tired. Feeling his pain yet falling dazed and sleepy, Parker felt he was lost of all energy. Submitting to his wounds, the peace and quiet made him slowly close his eyes. His eyelids became heavy. His breathing slowed down.

Then, he heard the distant sound of car tyres screeching.

Echoing throughout the car park. Again, and again. Each time, getting louder than the last time. The screeches made Parker open his eyes. Waking up one more time. With each sound of the tyres screeching, Parker knew who it was. The sounds made Parker's heart beat faster. Making his body come back into life.

His nerves were growing with the sound of the screeching tyres. Scared of seeing the person whose chase for him was coming to an end. Parker willed himself to get up off the floor. Struggling to stand up, he leaned his body against his car tyre. Placing a hand on it, he willed himself up to lean against the bonnet of his car.

Now standing on two feet, Jade's car arrived on the rooftop. Her car headlamps were shining straight in Parker's direction. The brightness made Parker squint his eyes. Even more so as the rain trickled down his head and face. Mixing together with the blood from the cut on his forehead. Parker wiped the water and blood from his eyes.

For a moment, Parker looked inside Jade's car. Staring her down eye to eye. Just like an old western gunfight waiting for the first shot to be fired.

Instantly, Jade sped her car fast towards Parker. Moving so fast, he had no time to move out of the way. Parker's body slammed hard on the front bonnet of Jade's car. His body is now lying on top. Briefly, still speeding forward, Jade saw Parker look at her through the car window. The bonnet was now wet from the rain. Jade quickly put her foot on the brake. Forcing Parker to slide off the bonnet. Collapsing once again on the concrete floor some several feet ahead of her.

Jade switched off the car engine. Leaving the light from her car headlamps on. Stepping out of her car with a gun in hand, Jade slowly approached Parker. She noticed him, with his good hand, holding a grip of his wounded shoulder.

Parker looked up at the powerful, domineering sight of Jade looking down on him. He looked deep into her eyes. Seeing the anger and passion raging within them. He saw no other emotion in the rest of her face. Her eyes were telling the whole story. Parker, beaten down, bloody and bruised, looked up at the woman who beat him in a game of cat and mouse.

'You must be Parker,' Jade said. 'Your friend back at the office told me a lot about you. But not enough.'

Taking a few steps forward, Jade kicked Parker's good hand away from his wound. She then placed the heel of her boot hard on his wound. Squeezing her boot down hard, she caused the pain to make Parker scream out aloud.

'Get up,' Jade demanded. She continued pressing down hard on his wound. Parker continued to scream. She knew all too well he could not get up.

'I SAID GET UP!' Jade screamed. But Parker screamed louder. Having no control over what he could or could not do. He was lying there helpless and pathetic.

Then Jade lifted up her heel from his wound. Giving Parker a mere second to breathe. Before then kicking the side of his head with her boot. Parker now felt dazed. She then kicked him several times in the stomach, lungs, and rib area. Jade moved around to spread his legs and stand between them.

'Now for the crown jewels,' she said.

Raising up her heel and boot, Jade slammed hard and fast down right onto Parker's manhood.

Making sure her sharp heel stabbed sharply into his testicles. Parker screamed out an almighty cry. 'You may have balls, but at least I don't have to think with them all the time,' Jade said.

As she finished her physical assault on Parker, Jade tightened her grip on her gun. She lowered herself down. Lifting Parker up with a tight grip on his shirt. She stared down into his beaten, red-shot eyes.

'Tell me what you know,' Jade said. 'Why did you do it? Why did you kill my son?'

'What I know won't bring him back,' replied Parker in his deep masculine voice.

'TELL ME! Were you paid to do it? Who told you to do it?'

'What difference will it make now? What's coming in the future? You can't stop it coming. This city will burn. The match is waiting to be lit.'

'You're doing my patience.'

'I'm just a hitman for hire who wears a good suit. I know nothing. Do I lie?' Parker began laughing.

Full of rage, Jade punched Parker hard in the face. Making his head fall back down onto the concrete floor.

Rising to her feet, Jade pointed her gun down at Parker's face. Ready to pull the trigger. Parker had a cocky, yet bloody, smile on his face. *Any second now,* he thought. *Any second.*

'JADE!'

She looked to see Tanner walking towards her nearby.

'Don't do this,' he said quietly.

'He killed my son,' Jade said as tears started falling down her face. 'And you weren't there at the hospital when I needed you.'

Tanner did not reply. He knew this was the wrong time to explain himself. Jade, not hearing a reply, looked back down at the cocky smiling Parker.

'Jade, please,' Tanner quietly said. 'Here we are again. Right back where we started. Same situation, just like all those years ago. I stopped you once before doing this. If I have to do it again to save you, I will. Don't do this, Jade. You kill him, and the police won't know what he's done. All they'll see is what you've done to him. Don't let him win. Make the right choice.'

Just then, slowly, Parker picked himself up off the floor.

116

Never losing eye contact with Jade, who kept her gun pointing at his head.

'Jade,' Parker said. 'You weren't strong enough to save him. Just like you are at pulling that trigger.' She stood silent. She turned and looked at Tanner.

'I'm not doing it for me,' Jade said to Tanner. 'This is for Sean.'

BANG!

Jade pulled the trigger. Shooting into Parker's head. Blowing Parker's brains out. The sound of the bullet echoed loud and long. Parker's corpse collapsed down onto the floor. Tanner stepped back, looking on in shock.

Jade lowered down her gun. She watched the blood pour out of Parker's head. The rain poured down, spreading the blood all around Parker's body.

Above Jade, a spotlight shone down on her and the surrounding area, including Parker's dead body.

Jade heard the sound of a helicopter from up above.

From the helicopter, Julius and Louis looked down at the bloody scene that had taken place on the rooftop. From what Julius could see, it was conclusive.

Jade is a cold blooded murderer.

Julius grabbed hold of a megaphone. Sliding the side helicopter door open, Julius spoke aloud into the megaphone. His voice being heard on the rooftop.

'This is the police. Put down your gun, Jade Hall. You are under arrest.'

Jade looked up at the spotlight. She let her gun fall out of her hand to the floor. She raised her hands up. Jade was fully aware that she had crossed the line. But after what these men had done to her son Sean, she did not care.

Jade had got what she wanted. The bastards were dead.

Chapter 21

Jade was being placed in the back of a police van. Sitting still and silently, she felt she was being judged wrongly by those in authority. Misunderstanding her motives. And effectively misunderstanding her. Jade looked up to see Louis approaching the open rear door.

As they looked at one another, neither of them said anything to the other. But by looking at the person's eyes, they read an understanding of the other. Louis understood how hurt and lost Jade felt in this moment.

Jade took comfort in knowing Louis knew the truth. Knowing he was still supportive of her and feeling sorry for her after the tragic loss and events she had gone through in the past few hours.

Just then, an officer approached. Asking Louis to step back from the open van door. As he did, Jade nor Louis took their eye off the other.

The only thing that stopped the eye contact was the rear police van door slamming shut.

Nearby, Tanner and Julius stood side by side, watching the police van being driven away from the scene of the crime. Julius took the chance to have a dig at his former friend.

'She was promising once, Frank,' Julius said sarcastically. 'Amazing how the mighty have fallen.'

'I didn't think she'd do it. Pull the trigger,' Tanner replied. 'But I believe in her. You only see her one way, Julius.

She can be more than that. She can be above that.'

'You'll never give up, will you Frank?' Julius asked.

Tanner gave no reply. He had seen enough. He walked away into the night. Alone.

Julius walked a few paces away. Wanting to be alone, he walked off to an area that was private, away from the police unit at the scene.

Taking out his mobile phone, he made a call. Waiting for it to be answered, he looked around to make sure he was still alone. When he knew his call was answered, he passed on his message.

'Hi. It's Julius. Parker and his associate are dead. But Jade Hall's been caught and arrested. I'll speak to you soon. Goodnight.'

*

Having reached Alpha City prison, Jade's belongings had now been taken from her. Stripped of her normal clothes, Jade was now wearing a standard jail shirt and trousers.

She was being escorted down a long corridor. In the cells left and right of her, criminals shouted and screamed out of their cells. Jade knew she was responsible for putting a lot of them in here. She knew she would have a target on her now. And she knew she was ready for them.

As the prison officer opened up a specific door, Jade walked into the cell. As the door slammed shut, Jade noticed another person already occupying the cell.

An older white-haired woman in her fifties. Once the woman noticed Jade enter the cell, she stood up from her chair next to a wooden desk.

The woman offered her hand out to Jade.

'It's okay I know who you are, Jade. Gossip spreads fast in this place,' the white-haired woman said.

Jade slowly raised her hand to shake the woman's hand. 'It's nice to meet you, Jade. My name is Eve.'

Chapter 22

As several weeks had passed by, Tanner was driving around the city late at night. Still pondering over recent events, Tanner could not shake off the thoughts of Jade and her son Sean. Feeling responsible for what had happened, pushing, and encouraging Jade to become a Private Detective, he started putting the pieces together in his head. After Farrell had been killed by Jade, Tanner knew it was Jack Kane who ordered the revenge attack. With Farrell now dead, Tanner knew the loss of Farrell put damage to Kane's plans and operations.

Concluding, Tanner had made his choice. He was heading towards Kane's territory.

With the power and strength behind him, the treaty signed declared that Kane would not leave Alpha Central, which he had business control over. Jack Kane had power over Alpha Central like a business conglomerate. But with Tanner being an independent Detective, it was difficult, but possible for him to come face to face with Kane. But for Tanner to do this, it was a huge risk for his safety and his life. Kane's territory was unsafe and unpredictable. He knew he was on his own.

Tanner drove down a stretch of city centre road made up of restaurants, clubs, pubs, strip joints, casinos, etc. Observing the nightlife, he saw the sight of drunks, drug takers, prostitutes standing on street corners. The streets and surrounding area were a mess. Filled with filth, grease, and dirt. Steam rises up through the grids from the city centre sewers.

Tanner stopped his car near an Italian restaurant called 'Godfathers.' Stepping out of the car, he knew this was one of the places Kane was most likely to be. There was a good chance, he thought, to find Kane here. Especially when he saw the familiar face of Tyson standing on guard by the restaurant entrance.

Tyson recognised Tanner walking up towards him. So, he stood in front of Tanner. Stopping him from entering the restaurant.

As they stared at each other, Tanner took out his gun and willingly offered it to Tyson. 'I've come to talk to your boss. Jack Kane,' Tanner said.

Feeling satisfied, Tyson took Tanner's gun away from him. 'Follow me,' Tyson ordered.

*

Inside, the restaurant was filled full of Kane's friends, accomplices, and business partners. Each taking up a table filled of women for their company.

Tanner knew they all wreaked of corruption, crime, and assassinations. But none had the power that Kane had.

Kane sat alone. Quietly eating his meal at a circular table placed in the centre of the restaurant. Reaching Kane's table, Tyson pulled back a chair for Tanner. Then, grabbing a strong hold of Tanner's shoulder, Tyson forced him viciously to sit down in the chair opposite Kane. Tyson stayed standing ominously behind Tanner.

Tanner stared at Kane. Waiting for him to say the first word. But Kane did not look up at Tanner.

He stayed focused on finishing his meal. As he did, he wiped

122

his hands and mouth with his handkerchief. He looked up at Tanner, remaining calm and composed.

'Have the police sent you as a friendly associate?' Kane asked.

'I've come alone. They don't know I'm here,' replied Tanner.

'That's unfortunate. And a very high risk to take, Frank. Am I right? You're Frank Tanner?'

'You know me?'

'I knew your father. Richard Tanner. He was a good private detective. And a good man, too. But like a lot of people in this city, your father disagreed with my methods of business. He was even an enemy to my boss. The man who taught me everything. Have you come here to tell me you disagree with my methods, too?'

'I think me and my partner sent a message when she killed your good friend Farrell.'

'Don't you mean your ex-partner, Frank? Jade, isn't it? She killed him and made me very angry by what she did. Now, in jail, she's paying the price for letting her heart rule her choices. Are you sad to see your protege crumble beneath you? You wanted to follow in your father's footsteps. You were his protege. Trained by him, too. And I bet you were afraid to crumble and fail. Maybe you did. Maybe you became the big disappointment of your father's life.'

Tanner knew what Kane was doing. He was touching a nerve and wanting to push his buttons.

Hoping Tanner would make a choice he would live to regret. But Tanner let his intellect take control. He changed tactics.

'After all that you've done,' Tanner said, 'you got control of Alpha Central. Why do you want full control of this city so bad?'

'Power, Frank,' Kane replied. 'Anybody can sit in a powerful chair. It's all a question of which building that chair is in. And I'm going to get it. And I'll tell you this. After all the fighting in recent weeks, including the big mess your friend Jade's been in, I'm calling a truce for now. You can send that back to the new Mayor, Paul Gordon. But the clock is ticking. And the seconds will run down. Then it'll be my turn for the ball to be in my court.'

'When will that happen?' Tanner asked.

'You'll know it when it arrives. Tyson, get him out of here.'

Instantly, Tyson grabbed hold of Tanner's coat. Forcing him to stand up from his chair. Kane kept his eyes on Tanner.

Tyson, with force, pushed Tanner back towards the main entrance. Making Tanner leave the restaurant.

Now alone at the table, Kane thought on what to do next. Thinking what his next line of attack would be.

Tyson, now alone, walked back towards Kane's table. 'So, what do we do now, sir?' Tyson asked.

'We've got Farrell's chemical formula. We'll continue with the plan. Send out the men, top secret, to collect and kidnap the wealthiest families' children. All the children from all over the city. Hold them for ransom. And threaten to kill them with Farrell's fatal cocktail. And we'll start the plan tonight.'

'Are you sure, sir? We'll be crossing outside Alpha Central to get them.'

'I'm sure. The time is right. We have to strike while the iron is hot. Start making plans.'

'Yes, sir.'

Tyson began walking away. But Kane had another thought. 'Tyson!'

'Yes, sir.' Tyson stopped walking so he could hear Kane's

next command.

'Find out all you can on Frank Tanner and his past,' Kane ordered. 'Find out any useful information on him. I want to know what secrets he has hidden away.'

Chapter 23

The following day, Jade sat alone at a table in the prison canteen having a meal. Looking up at the T.V placed high on a shelf in the corner of the room near the ceiling. She watched a local news report on news and events taking place in other cities around the country.

'Reports from around the country show anarchy and attacks being made by a new unnamed terrorist group,' the reporter said. 'Alpha City's threat level has been raised to severe in response to potential attacks being made within the city. I spoke to Mayor Paul Gordon to get his response.'

As Mayor Gordon came on screen, he looked like your typical politician. In his late thirties, he had slim, brown hair, wearing a formal suit and tie. He spoke in a formal way that lacked a sense of sincerity with the authority he had. This was a drawback for Mayor Gordon. Having been trained to respond in such a manner, it did not, however, raise confidence, trust or belief from the city population watching him. Jade being one of them. Nevertheless, Mayor Gordon responded as best he could to the attacks taking place across the country.

'It is imperative that this threat does not bleed into the hope we aim to achieve in our great city. I promise you these attacks will not reach our city and rip apart further the good work we have done to unite our city once again. That is our goal.'

'You say that, Mister Mayor, but does Jack Kane share those values with you?' the reporter replied. 'You talk of a city united, but it looks like a city more divided now than ever.'

'Well, let me just say about Jack Kane that if these terrorists started attacking his section of the city, I'm confident he would search for my help and need in response to such attacks. Yes, we are on different sides of the divide right now, but if these attacks threaten us all, I would consider talking to Jack Kane and offer my support if ever he needed it. Until then, the divisions will remain in place between his side and ours. But I believe this city will unite as one when we share a common enemy.'

'So, the enemy of your enemy is your friend?'

'Let me put it this way: *I* would unite with anyone to fight against those who threaten our city by any means necessary. Those alliances may not be popular by some, but for the greater good, I will do what is needed for the good of the city. Thank you very much.' With that, Mayor Gordon walked away from the reporter. Waving to the nearby cameras and photographers.

In the canteen, Eve walked up to Jade's table and sat down opposite her. She placed her glass and plate on the table. Ready to start eating her meal. She, too, had been watching the same report on TV.

'Mayor Gordon hasn't got a clue what he's talking about,' Eve said.

'How do you mean?' Jade asked.

'He doesn't know who the real enemy is. Kane? Maybe. Or it might be those that stay in the shadows. Waiting. Waiting for the right moment to step out into the light and strike. Without warning. The enemy he cannot see until they want you to see them.'

'So, who is the real enemy?' Jade asked.

'Tekker. When they step into the light, they'll stay there. And when they do, only then will everyone know how strong a group they are. They always leave their mark wherever they go. Gordon can't stop them from coming to this city. The clock's ticking. Tekker will strike. And she'll be wanting to take this city for herself.'

'What do you mean?' Jade asked. 'Who is she?'

Before Eve could reply, Jade's ear picked up more of the ongoing news report that was on the T.V. 'In other news, a series of child kidnappings have taken place across Alpha City in the past twelve hours. Currently, six children have been reported missing, with early reports sketchy at best.'

As Jade listened on, her mind and thoughts became more focused. Eve became concerned for her friend.

'Jade? What's wrong?'

'It's starting again,' Jade replied.

'What is?'

'I need to speak to the chief warden.'

Jade stood up from her chair. Walking fast, she was walking out of the canteen with purpose.

*

A few minutes later, Jade was being escorted by two prison officers down a long, cold, white-bricked corridor. Reaching the chief warden's office door at the far end, Jade knocked on the door, opened it and walked in.

As she entered, she was slightly taken aback by who she saw in the room, for it was not the chief warden but a familiar face standing looking out of the office window down onto the prison courtyard.

He turned and looked at Jade. Giving a warm, sincere smile. Hoping it would give her comfort to see an old face.

'Louis,' Jade said.

'Jade. It's good to see you.'

'Have you been promoted from the police force?'

'No. I've come to escort you.'

'Why? Where are we going?'

'For a little trip.'

*

Sometime later, Jade sat with Louis in the back of a police car. Leaving the prison, Jade could not help but have a sense of excitement. Being able to leave the place she thought she would spend the rest of her life within.

Turning to look at Louis, she had to admit she was happy to see him. She felt she should say something.

'Thanks for the letters,' she said quietly.

'You're welcome. I can imagine it's been tough for you in there. I thought the letters of support would help.'

'They did. I'm very grateful, Louis.'

He nodded his head in appreciation of Jade's comment. Then he turned to look back up ahead.

Gesturing towards Jade that, they had arrived. 'Here we are,' he said.

Jade looked up ahead. Seeing a building she was very familiar with. Alpha City Town Hall.

*

Jade and Louis walked alone down a long, polished, wooden, varnished, well-dressed formal corridor. Neither one said anything to the other. Louis was leading Jade towards a specific door with the name of 'MAYOR PAUL GORDON' engraved on it.

Jade stared at the engraved name as Louis opened the door. She was the first to step through the open door, followed by Louis, who closed the door behind him.

The office was large with big windows to the right looking down onto the large city square outside. The room was clean, polished and varnished. Light bouncing off the clean wooden floor. Carpet covering the area in front of Jade, with a large desk ahead of her.

At the desk were two chairs nearest Jade facing the desk with the mayors chair the opposite side facing towards her.

Looking around the edge of the room, Jade saw paintings and portraits of events and people important in the history of the city. As her eyes scanned the large room, she saw yet another familiar face standing looking out of the window. A face she was not that comfortable to see.

Tanner, she thought. *My former friend.*

Chapter 24

'Good that you arranged to see me after all this time,' Jade said sarcastically. She was smart enough to know Tanner had arranged nothing of the sort.

'Actually,' Louis replied, 'both of you were asked to come to this meeting.'

'I know Louis. All too well what Tanner hasn't been doing.'

Jade stared right at Tanner. He had not moved an inch or said anything. His expression not changing one bit.

Not one phone call, Jade thought. *Not even one letter. No visits from you. No contact whatsoever from you, Frank.*

Jade wanted to shake the thought from her mind. She started walking off casually around the room, looking at the paintings and ornaments placed on the side tables around the edge of the room.

'Well, it's not rocket science to know whose office I'm in,' Jade said. 'The name on the door gives it away. So come on. Where are you?'

At that moment, the door opened. Stepping into the room was Mayor Gordon, followed by Julius Carver.

'I'm here, Miss Hall,' said Mayor Gordon.

Gordon approached to shake Jade's hand. She refused to take it. She took several steps back away from Gordon. Clearly sending a message of a lack of trust in Gordon, which he duly noted. Accepting her response, Gordon turned his attention to

131

Tanner. Walking over to the window, he offered his hand out for Tanner.

'Mister Tanner, glad you could come,' Gordon said as he shook Tanner's hand freely.

As Tanner shook Gordon's hand, he looked over at Jade. Both making eye contact, and yet both uncomfortable looking at the other. Tanner turned his attention back to Gordon.

'I'm happy to be of service, Mister Mayor,' Tanner said letting go of Gordon's hand.

Gordon started walking around to his desk to sit down behind it. Julius followed on, not far behind.

As Julius passed Tanner, the two former friends made brief eye contact before Julius walked on to stand behind Mayor Gordon, looking over his shoulder.

'Would you both like to sit down?' Gordon said, gesturing towards Jade and Tanner.

Both walked and sat down towards the two chairs on the other side of the mayor's desk. Louis positioned himself to stand directly behind Jade. He was, after all, still on duty with Jade in his custody.

'Thank you both for agreeing to come here,' Gordon said.

'Better than staring through metal bars,' replied Jade.

'Yes. Murder Miss Hall? Am I right?' asked Gordon. 'Julius has brought me up to speed.'

'Really?' Jade looked up at Julius. Someone she had grown to disagree with and be in conflict with in the past. 'Tell me, did catching me get you one step closer to that promotion?'

'Miss Hall, Julius was doing his job. Aiming to keep the peace. Based on your recent actions, I could question your professionalism,' Gordon said.

'Tell you what,' Jade said, 'why don't I kill all your loved ones? And let's see if you're driven to do the same as I did. I carried my son inside me for nine months. A creation sacred only for a woman to know, feel and experience. For my son to be killed, it ripped me apart. As a parent, you'd do anything to take down those responsible. If you don't understand that point, you know nothing about what I've been through. Compared to my son, staying professional was the last thing on my mind. So, don't you dare offend me about being professional? Being a mother, that's for life.'

Gordon gave no reply. Nor did any of the other men present. After all, for a mother to lose her child was something none of them could relate to.

Changing gear, Gordon knew he had to ask Jade a question that was going to touch a personal nerve.

'You're an orphan. Aren't you, Miss Hall?' Gordon asked.

Gordon could tell in her facial reaction she was somewhat uncomfortable by being asked that question.

'Yes. Yes, I am,' replied Jade.

'What does it feel like to be alone?' Gordon asked.

'Very quiet,' she replied sarcastically.

'But not in your heart. You can't stop how being an orphan makes you feel. It's part of your makeup. Makes you be the person you are.'

'What about it?' Jade asked.

'What was your aim when you became a private detective?' asked Gordon.

'To help others. And not have others suffer the way I did.'

'Even a child, Miss Hall?'

'Especially a child.'

'There were two children you didn't save. One was captured by Farrell. The other being your own son. Would you like to redeem yourself from those mistakes?'

'If offered the choice,' Jade said. 'Yes.'

'Good. Well, here's my offer.' Gordon sat up straight in his chair, placing the palms of his hands on his desk.

'The children that have disappeared in the past twelve hours,' he said. 'Find them. Both you and Tanner. If my instincts are correct, there's a chance the children could've been taken into Kane's city territory. Places the police cannot afford to go. Unless they want a civil war on their hands with Kane as their enemy.'

'If I find them, what will happen to me?' Jade said. 'Do I get a pat on the back, a thank you and then pushed back behind prison bars?'

'I'll give you a full pardon for your actions,' Gordon declared. Julius looked stunned as he was hearing this for the first time.

'You give your word on that, Mayor Gordon?' Jade said.

'My official word as Mayor of this city,' he replied.

Jade looked up at the silent Julius standing behind the mayor. Jade noticed that Julius looked uncomfortable at the offer the mayor had just given to her. Jade looked back at Gordon to speak to him.

'Is Julius, your police friend, happy with this offer of a pardon?'

'He'll have to be,' replied Gordon. 'Julius maintains the law in his own way. I make the law my way. So, do we have a deal?'

Jade sat silently. Not yet giving her reply.

'You'd make an alliance and trust yourself to a killer?' Jade asked.

'Sometimes we need allies who are willing to pull the trigger,' replied Gordon. 'We all need allies. Both you and me.

I'll trust you to do your job because of your orphaned, maternal past. You can trust my word because of the threats that are heading our way. The attacks on our city and its future from people like Kane. Our children are our future.'

'Without my child, what's my future?' Jade asked.

'Do you wish other parents to ask the same question? The parents of those children that are out there somewhere? Do you?'

Jade gave no reply. She knew deep down that Gordon was right. Deep down, there was a shred of a decent human being still within Jade. She wanted to fight for good. And not wanting others to have the pain that Jade knew all too well about. She wanted to do the right thing. She wanted to feel like herself again. She wanted the real Jade to come back.

Slowly, Jade nodded her head for yes. A deal had been struck. Taking from her gesture that they were now in alliance, Mayor Gordon sat back comfortably in his chair.

'You can leave the prison with immediate effect,' said Gordon. 'You'll be put under Tanner's custody until further notice. You can begin work when you're both ready.'

Hearing Tanner's name mentioned finally, Jade turned to take a glimpse of Tanner's face beside her.

'You haven't said much, have you?' Jade said towards Tanner.

'He didn't need to,' replied Gordon. 'He'd already had a private meeting with me earlier. He persuaded me to give you another chance. He's the reason you're here being given this offer.'

'Why am I being treated with so much care?' asked Jade.

'Because you've shown you're still inexperienced, raw, and emotionally driven. Both myself and Tanner feel there's more to you than that. I think you would like to prove a point that there is.'

'Prove a point to who?' she said. 'You and Tanner?'

'No. To prove a point for yourself, Miss Hall.'

Jade pondered on Gordon's last comment. As she did, Gordon stood up from his chair. 'Thank you all for your time today. Frank, Louis, Miss Hall.'

Gordon walked around his desk to shake Tanner's hand. Once again, he offered his hand out for Jade to shake.

She ignored the gesture. Instead, she stood up from her chair and walked out of the mayor's office escorted by Louis.

Whilst Gordon finished the formalities of saying farewell to Tanner, Julius stayed standing behind the mayor's chair. Pondering on the decisions the mayor had just made in the meeting.

Julius now had matters of his own to be concerned about. Thinking back to his past dealings and encounter with Jack Kane, his connections to arrange helping Farrell escape prison, and then turning his back on his deal with Kane. He knew these events could possibly cause trouble for him at some point down the road. But with Jade now in alliance with Mayor Gordon, Jade was about to become a thorn in his side. He knew Jade well enough to know if she found out about him helping Farrell and his deal with Kane, she would be hungry to dig deeper.

Possibly leading Jade towards evidence relating to Julius' past corrupt background within the police force. Julius was now in troubled waters. Thanks to Mayor Gordon's decisions, life could start to be more uncomfortable for Julius and his allies.

As Tanner left the office, leaving Julius alone with the Mayor, Julius portrayed his concern in a professional manner towards Gordon. All the time, he is masking his true feelings.

'Mister Mayor, are you really sure about this? Making an alliance with a cold-hearted murderer like Jade Hall? Wc investigated the two men she murdered. We found nothing on them. I don't believe they were behind the death of her son. She murdered them in cold blood.'

'Julius, these are desperate times we live in,' replied Gordon. 'There are darker clouds than Jade Hall coming our way. The enemy of my enemy is my friend. We need her.'

'Sir, what do you mean by darker clouds? How do you know what's coming?' asked Julius.

'Professional intuition. Nothing more. You can go.'

Julius started walking towards the office door. Opening it, he took one last glance at Mayor Gordon and then left the office, closing the door behind him.

Now all alone, Gordon slowly walked towards his office window. Looking out into the square below, Gordon was full of concern and worry, with one thought circling around in his mind over and over again.

I truly wish it was nothing more than intuition.

*

Outside in the corridor, Julius walked alone. Now, a few hundred yards away from the mayor's office, Julius took out his mobile phone. Still walking. He was typing out a new text on his phone. It read 'JADE IS OUT. WORKING FOR THE MAYOR WITH TANNER.'

Once he had finished typing, he pressed send. Sending a new text to an ally. Satisfied, Julius left the town hall and headed back to police headquarters.

Chapter 25

A few hours had passed. Jade was back in her prison cell. Packing her belongings into a large plastic bag.

Alone by herself, Jade quietly pondered on her thoughts. The most dominant thought being that of her son, Sean. Seeing him smile and imagining him in a playground. Watching the childhood innocence that was a part of him. Jade continued on, trying to focus her thoughts on the memory of his voice. It had become important to her to remember his voice in her mind. In some way, feeling that by doing this, she was still connected to him. Feeling he was still there. Of course, being a mother, she always will be connected to him. But now he was gone, she felt it was her spiritual mission to hold onto him in her mind and soul. Now everything else of him was now gone, that meant more to her than anything else.

Several minutes went by. Someone tapped on the open cell door. Jade turned to see Eve standing there in the doorway. Eve smiled but felt envious looking at Jade.

'So, I hear we're losing a prison mate?' Eve said.

On hearing Eve's voice, Jade stopped what she was doing. She turned to give Eve her full attention.

'I've been given a chance, Eve,' Jade said. 'A chance to redeem myself.

'I don't blame you for taking it. But could you live with yourself if you fail again?'

'I don't know.'

'We all have to make choices. And we all have to live by them.'

'I've made my choice, Eve. I'll live by it. That's a promise I won't walk away from.'

As Jade finished speaking, Eve approached her. Placing her arms around her and embracing her.

Giving Jade a sincere, caring hug.

For Jade, it was the first sincere affection or care she had felt in many years. Jade felt an odd sensation. She was not use to being given such a simple gesture of a hug. Yet she felt Eve's sincerity of caring through how she was holding Jade in her arms. Jade took the chance to hold and embrace Eve in her arms, too. Her own care and friendly affection for Eve had grown in the period of time they had spent together. The one regret Jade had of taking the offer given was the sadness of having to leave someone she now considered a friend. The friend she never had growing up. Maybe even the mother she never had growing up.

As the two gently let go of the other, they both knew this was the last moment they would have together. With that, Eve gave one last comment. A simple defiant belief in knowing who it was standing in front of her. The strong woman standing in front of her.

'Goodbye, Jade. Goodbye, Jade Hall.'

*

An hour later, after going through her official release papers, Jade was in a car, finally leaving prison. As a passenger, she had Tanner as her driver.

Sat in the front passenger seat, Jade did not look his way. Instead, she preferred to look out of the window. Taking in the sights of the city she had not properly seen in quite some time.

Even as he drove, Tanner still felt the urge to glance over at Jade. Hoping she would look over and make eye contact with him. Maybe even to help break the silence. But it never came. Jade was preoccupied with looking at the sights of the city. Feeling a sense of nostalgia for a city landscape she yearned to connect back to.

Tanner was now feeling more uncomfortable. He felt it was right to make the first move in making conversation.

'I'm sorry I didn't come to see you. I can't imagine how hard it's been for you recently.'

'Take a wild guess,' Jade said whilst still looking out of the window.

'After all that's happened, I don't know what to say.'

On hearing that comment, Jade instantly turned to face Tanner.

'I know what to say,' Jade said. 'You were there for me when Sean was born. Why weren't you there for me when he died?'

'I was,' replied Tanner. 'I stood outside the hospital room. The room Sean was in. I saw you go in, but I was scared. Scared of not knowing what to do. Not knowing what choice was the right choice.'

'When your back is pushed up against the wall, you find out the truth in a lot of people,' Jade said. 'The truth in knowing who your real friends and loved ones are. I needed you then. The moment my whole world crumbled and fell apart. I needed you more than ever.'

'I know. And I'm sorry. I was ashamed. Ashamed of pushing this life on you. Encouraging you to be what you are now. Letting you be in the private detective world you're now in. For all that,

140

I blame myself that you lost Sean. I failed you and him. Jade, I'm so sorry I let you down.'

Jade gave no reply to Tanner. Instead, she turned to look up ahead out of the window. 'Jade, please. Say something,' Tanner pleaded.

'Pull over.'

'What?'

'I said pull over. Now!'

Tanner slowed the car to a stop. Pulling over by the side of the road. Turning his attention to Jade, he waited for her to speak.

'I want to be alone,' she said.

'Jade, let me take care of you.'

'I can take care of myself. I've been doing it my whole life. Just give me time to think things over.'

Having a moment to take things in, Tanner felt it was fair to let Jade be given her own space for the time being.

'If you need me, you know where to find me,' Tanner said.

Just then, a faint glimmer of care for Tanner came over Jade. She felt the need to reassure him. 'I swear on Sean's soul I won't run away. I'll see you soon,' she said.

Jade opened the door, stepped out, closed the door shut and started walking away from the car down the street.

Tanner sat back in his seat, looking on at Jade. Through all she had been through, he still looked on at Jade in admiration. Her posture, stance and walk gave signs she was still that tough, strong woman he knew her to be. Maybe it was her shield to protect her vulnerable, scarred heart.

Whatever the case, Tanner trusted Jade. And as he drove away, he knew that wouldn't be the last time he would see her.

Chapter 26

Jade walked alone with her thoughts. Daydreaming and thinking of the effect all the events would now have on her heavy heart. Feeling the pain from the loss she now lived with. She knew what lay within. All those scars, hurt and loss. But she knew something more brewing deeper within her.

Something feeding on all the bad that has happened to her. A demon? Maybe. A dark emotion?

Jade did not know. But she knew it was smiling and laughing at her. A laugh she could not shake off. Jade had to shut off this feeling. Focusing back on Sean and the love she had for him. The only person she ever knew who truly made Jade feel most like herself and who she was meant to be.

She continued walking. Distracting herself from her deepest feelings. She was walking past a nearby playground. Seeing children having fun, playing and being friends with other children.

Seeing them was a refreshing sight for Jade. Making her fully wake up from her deepest and darkest thoughts. The children had made her feel a sense of calm again within her. Now, only realising how deep in thought she had been, she had forgotten how many miles she had walked.

Getting her bearings, she looked around the surrounding area. It all seemed very familiar to her. Suddenly, it hit her. She knew all too well the block of flats that stood near her. As she looked up, she could see an opening in the block. The opening had black markings around the rough edges.

Made from the explosion that blasted out from inside the flat.

My home, Jade thought.

*

Jade reached the closed door to her former flat. She stood still. Slightly nervous. Staring at the door. She had not been back to the flat since the day of the explosion. The day that took away her child's life.

Gently placing her hand on the door, she pushed it open with ease and stepped inside.

Although it was her home, she barely recognised it. Faint traces of the wallpaper, carpeting, beds were still there that she was familiar with.

Wind from the large opening made from the explosion rushed through the flat and corridor where Jade now stood.

The walls were covered in black burnt marks. The carpet is full of ash, dirt, rubble, and wood.

Scattered everywhere throughout the flat. The ash is being blown in the wind.

Approaching the door threshold to the living room, Jade looked to see the large outer opening made from the bomb. Taking a few steps forward, she looked out of the opening towards the city. She knew she was standing where Sean was at the time of the explosion. The room is now a mess and totally destroyed. Nearby, she could see Sean's toys, which he liked to play with. Half buried under dirt and ash. Some plastic toys melted and burnt as well.

She began to imagine the memories in this room from years gone by. She could see herself in her mind's eye with Sean.

Memories that were now ghosts in time. Her emotions were starting to build up within her.

She imagined hearing echoes of Sean's laughter and voice in her mind. But she imagined them coming from another room. Jade turned away, walking back down the corridor towards the bedroom door. Opening it, this would have been Sean's bedroom.

The room still had remnants of the child-themed wallpaper and bed. Toys scattered all over the floor. Looking into the room, a tear fell down the cheek on Jade's face.

Once again, she could imagine seeing the memories of herself with Sean in this room. Playing games, reading him a bedtime story, singing him a lullaby whilst he was asleep in his cot. So many memories rushing through her mind.

She slowly walked into the centre of the room. Circling around, her emotions were dominating her every second.

Then, looking down at the floor, her eye was attracted to the edge of a small photo frame. Dust and ash covered over most of the frame, hiding the photo underneath. As Jade lowered down to pick it up, the ash and dust slid off the frame.

Inside the frame, the glass was cracked in several places. But behind it lay a photo of Jade and Sean together, smiling, and happy, with Jade holding Sean in her arms.

Her eyes turned red. Filled with tears, they started running down her face. Jade could not hold it in any more. She wept, making no effort to wipe away the tears.

She placed the photo tight to her chest. Holding tight and embracing it. Closing her eyes, she collapsed on the floor. Sobbing endlessly. The feeling of heartbreak stronger than ever before. Her emotions crumbling and falling apart within her.

In that moment, Jade felt so lost, so alone and so empty.

I miss my boy; she repeated in her thoughts. Again, and again.

Her tears continued until there was no more to give. Her eyes began to dry but remained bloodshot red from the emotion. Jade slowly started to breathe in and out. Beginning to calm herself down and bring her back from the saddest of emotional places to be in.

Opening her eyes, she looked up. Placing the photo frame in front of her, she gently kissed it.

Moving it away from her face, she looked at the photo. Now, having all that powerful emotion out of her system, she could finally look at the photo. Remembering the love she had for Sean when the photo was taken. As well as the love he had for her. As his mother.

'Jade,' a young voice said nearby.

She turned, looking back at the doorway. A familiar teenage face stood there with a look of care and concern on his face.

'Luke,' replied Jade. She rose and picked herself up off the floor.

'I heard you were out of prison. I thought you might come here,' he said.

'I had to. I couldn't stay away. This was my home. How did you know I was out?'

'Word spreads fast in this city. I wanted to see you.'

'Why?' Jade asked curiously.

'To say thank you. For what you did for me. Finding the person who killed my friend. And also helping me look after the other homeless residents in Alphaville. I didn't get the chance to properly tell you that before.'

After hearing what Luke said, Jade felt he had been a

godsend. Helping to lift her up. Reassuring her at the most painful of moments. Luke's words reminded Jade of the memory, effort, and strength to get the job done. And getting it done successfully. Reminding her that in the past, she had made a difference. Now it was all about finding again that person within her to rise up and be strong for the sake of others.

'You're welcome, Luke,' replied Jade. 'I wish I could do that more of the time.'

'You could if you believe in yourself.' Luke smiled at Jade. He believed in her. He wanted her to be that person again.

Luke finally looked around the flat. Scanning the rooms with his eye. Looking down the hallway towards the living room.

'So, this is where it happened,' he said. 'The bomb that killed your son?' Jade nodded her head for yes.

'Who did this?' Luke asked.

'It was the man who was backing Farrell,' replied Jade. 'Farrell, the one who kidnapped the young children?' Luke said.

'Yes. I think the man backing him was the one who gave the bombers the job.'

'Who?'

'Jack Kane. All I need to do is find him.'

'That'll be tough,' Luke replied. 'Word is he's not been seen in Alpha Central for the past few days. We can only guess where to find him. It's like looking for a needle in a haystack. He could be anywhere.'

'Maybe he's starting to plan something big. So where shall I start?' Jade asked.

'Here's a good place.' Luke handed Jade a small note. Written on it was a name and address that Jade was already familiar with.

'You know him?' Luke said.

'Yeah. He's moved up the food chain fast. I'm impressed. How did you come by this?'

'From one of my contacts,' Luke replied. 'I've got many across the city Jade. They're here for me. And I'm here for you. Whenever you need me.'

Jade was impressed. She smiled at Luke. Admiring his effort to have a network of people in the city to rely on.

So, Jade thought, *I have a young sidekick working the streets.*

Chapter 27

As day turned into night over Alpha City and its skyline, Jade picked up her old black car out of storage. She was now making her way into Alpha Central.

Small trickles of rain began to fall. City lights bouncing off the wet reflections along the concrete roads and paths. Jade turned on her car window wipers.

Looking out her side car window, the pavements were packed full of people. Enjoying the nightlife of the city. She saw a mixture of drunkenness, laughter, and fun. Fights spilling out into the street outside pubs and nightclubs.

Yet Jade did not stop. She was on a mission. Continuing down the road, she saw more of the same as she passed. A recurring image of the same party life from similar bars, clubs, and restaurants. A large herd of people. A crowd where individuals lost their identity in the crowd of excess.

Jade was heading towards Chinatown. The small section of the city centre was lit up bright with neon lights decorating the exterior of popular restaurants. Decor of Chinese culture lining up alongside the streets. Ranging from painted dragons to Chinese words, when translated, meant peace, harmony, and love.

Tonight was a busy night for this section of the city. The crowds of people are too many to stay on the paths. Several of them were forced to walk out onto the road. Many getting in front of Jade's car. Turning off onto a street called George Street, Jade could see up ahead the neon-lit outline of the venue she was looking for. The neon light at the side of the entrance was shaped to emphasise the shape of a woman's body. Emphasising her breasts and figure. Jade had found the gentleman's club she was looking for called 'Temptations'.

She pulled up her car and switched off the engine, opposite the entrance to 'Temptations'. Stepping out of the car, Jade spotted a tall, built-up, bald security guard standing by the side of the club's entrance. The security guard looked over at Jade. Their eyes met. Jade was determined. The guard was curious to know what she was going to do next.

Jade started walking across the road towards the entrance. The guard had not taken his eyes off her. He was half curious to know what she was doing here, but also attracted by how beautiful she looked. She started walking towards the entrance. As she did, the tall security guard stepped out in front of her. Blocking her from entering the club.

'Get out of my way, big man,' Jade demanded, looking up at the tall security guard.

'This isn't your kind of club, love,' the guard replied.

'Really?' Jade pondered on her next thought of what to do next. 'Tell you what I'll do,' Jade said. 'Do you like having your balls?'

'Why?' the guard asked with both curiosity and worry.

Just then, Jade got out her gun and pointed it directly at the guards' groin.

'Because in three seconds,' Jade said, 'You won't have to think with them any more.'

The guard nervously and slowly stepped aside. Allowing Jade to enter the club. Placing her gun away, Jade gave one last comment to the guard.

'At least your crown jewels made you see sense in the end. Where will I find, Wayne Lao?'

'He'll be at the bar, miss,' the guard replied.

'Thank you, Incredible Hulk.'

*

As Jade entered the club, she made her way down a darkly lit staircase. Faintly lit along the walls by dark blue lighting. Creating a dark ambience of the club she was in.

Down below, she could hear the sound of loud pop music booming out into the gentleman's lounge. The songs that were playing were a medley of Freddie Mercury's solo songs like *Love Kills*, *Living on my Own (remix)* and Queen songs like *Body Language*, *Back Chat* and *Staying Power*.

Reaching the bottom of the staircase, Jade was standing by the small reception desk. The area was still darkly lit blue. The only other light was coming from a desk lamp shining down onto the desk.

The receptionist was waiting to take money from Jade as an entrance fee. Instead, Jade showed her private detective badge. The receptionist gestured at Jade that she could enter the club. Jade leaned in to ask the receptionist where she could find the bar. Once given directions, Jade turned to enter the main section of the club.

The club remained darkly lit but brighter than where Jade had just been. Spotlights were scattered around. Shining directly down on where they stood. One shining down on a nearby pool table. Several shining down each on an area of tables and black leather chairs. The main spotlight is on a dancing circular stage with a metal pole as its centrepiece.

A group of men were playing pool. Having as company a group of scantily clad, lingerie-wearing young black, white or Asian women who were strippers. Other such women were sat down, each with individual men scattered around the club.

A new stripper was beginning to perform on the main circular stage. Whilst others were leading the men in their company towards a nearby spiralling staircase. Leading up to the next level, where the men could pay for their own private dance in a private booth with their chosen woman.

Jade remained focused on why she was there. Looking for the person called Wayne Lao, she could see the bar nearby. Just then, she spotted Wayne sitting on a tall stool by the bar. Sandwiched between two scantily clad ladies. His arm round each of them.

Sat with his back to Jade, he was laughing away. Telling a few jokes to the women whilst also taking a swig from his chosen drink.

As Jade approached him, she tapped him hard on his shoulder. As he turned, Wayne remained smiling. But once he saw who was standing behind him, his smile dropped so fast from his face. Feeling he had been caught, Wayne started to sweat and go into a state of panic.

'Jade. Oh God,' Wayne said.

'My old friend,' Jade said with a sarcastic smile.

'I've done nothing wrong. I swear. This place is licensed and everything.'

'Really? Well, I'm not here to throw you back in the cell. I was given your name as someone who could help me.'

'Help? I'm happy to help you, Jade. Always,' Wayne anxiously said to reassure her.

'Get rid of the women. We need to talk.'

151

'Ladies,' Wayne commanded. The two ladies walked away towards a man who had just entered the club.

'Where can we chat?' Jade asked.

'This way.' Wayne gestured towards an office door at the far end of the club.

As Jade walked ahead, followed by Wayne, without her seeing, he gestured a nod to his nearby tall, bearded security guard. The guard gestured back at Wayne. The gesture from Wayne had given a command to the guard. With Wayne walking on behind Jade, the guard began preparing his next course of action.

Chapter 28

'Take a seat,' Wayne said as he opened the door to his main office.

Jade looked around the darkly lit room. Black padded walls. A spotlight shining down on his desk and chair, as well as an accompanying chair the side of the desk nearest Jade.

The desk shone of glossy wood. To her left, a closed large cupboard wooden door. To her right was a large wall-size glass window. Stretching the height and width of the office looking out into the club at the men and women.

'They can't see us. It's a double-sided window. On their side, it's just a mirror,' Wayne said as he poured himself a drink at a small bar placed in the corner of the room.

'Is this your private place where you can jerk off over the women that work for you?' asked Jade. Wayne looked nervous and gave no reply to Jade's question.

That would be a yes, Jade thought.

Wayne was a small Asian man. Around five feet tall. Wearing a good, clean suit and in his mid-forties. He looked very professional in his image. Yet he carried with him a nervous disposition. His character having an air of cowardice by nature but then turning powerfully cocky when the moment suited him.

Right now, he was mopping his brow. A nervous result of being in Jade's company. For Jade, his nervousness may have come from the memory of how strongly Jade dealt with him by putting him in jail. Or maybe it went deeper than that. Jade had a faint thought that deep down, Wayne was attracted to her and expressing his nerves may be a reflection of his shyness to express himself. Somewhere in Wayne lay the truth. He respected her and Jade trusted him. She knew he did not want to get on the wrong side of her again. And for that, Jade knew Wayne would tell her the truth to anything she would ask him.

'So, whilst I was in prison, you were building new ventures for yourself with this place?' Jade asked.

Wayne, now holding a glass in his hand, slowly walked around his desk to sit down. 'How did you find me here?' Wayne said.

'A reliable source. I'm impressed, Wayne. You went from a jailbird to a junkie. Then to a businessman in no time at all.'

'That's right, Jade. Alpha City is full of opportunities now. I started this place up only recently. Did you enjoy yourself in prison?'

'Why? Were you thinking of me?'

'I wondered what you got up to. Yes. I know what it's like being in there. Beaten up from pillar to post. But I served my time. Just like you.'

'And then you got hooked on the drugs, Wayne. Strange. I'm wondering how you went from drug addict scraping for money to then being able to buy this place.'

Wayne was now wary of Jade's suspicions about him.

'I swear, Jade. I've done nothing wrong. In this world, I'm no one important. I'm just a little man.'

'No. You're a little man with lots of big information. You hear, see, and know a lot of things. Don't take me for an idiot.'

'I don't, Jade. Believe me.' Then, a thought came to Wayne. 'Wait a minute. The kids that went missing recently. That's why you're here? I don't know where they are.'

Instantly, Jade stormed up to his desk, looking down on Wayne in his chair.

'I've read the police files,' Jade said. 'At each location, traces of a Z-listed drug were found on each child's bed. The kidnapper intoxicated them with a small dose of the drug. You had your contacts you could go to and get your drugs from. You know who would supply which drugs. So, who do you know that plays around with Z-listed drugs?'

'Farrell,' replied Wayne. 'But he's dead.'

'I know he's dead. I was the last person he saw alive. Do you want me to be the last person you see alive? Because your life is leaning that way if you don't tell me.'

'Would you allow me a last request?'

'Just tell me where I can find the person who now deals with these drugs.'

'Why?'

'Because if I find the drugs, I'll find Kane,' Jade said.

'Jack Kane? You're going after Kane? You're mad, Jade.'

'I might be mad. But I know how much you love me,' Jade said with a softer tone and flirty look in her eye.

Wayne was easily wooed by her speech, her charm and tone in her voice. Surprisingly, it began to calm Wayne down in her company. He slowly took a deep breath in and out before he began to speak.

'There's a rumour making the rounds in the past few hours. Kane has men secretly scattered all over Alpha City.'

'What are they doing?' Jade asked.

'Apparently, they plan on raiding the city chemists and medical supplies. Moving them all to a secret location.'

'What does he plan to do with it?'

'Ransom the city either by killing all the children kidnapped

155

or destroying all medicines needed for the people in the city. He's got hold of the medical records of the local hospitals. He knows they don't have the budget to replenish the stock required. He's started to tighten his grip on power for the city. And he's ready to make the next big expansion of his business empire.'

'So, he has the children?'

Wayne nodded his head for yes. 'Where are they?' Jade asked.

'I don't know where they are. I swear. If I knew, I would tell you Jade. Wait. Wait a minute.'

Wayne leant up from his chair. Writing down an address on a piece of paper, he slid the paper across his desk towards Jade.

'What's this?' Jade said.

'My sources said they've spotted a lot of men going into that building today. Men known for being paid by Jack Kane. Apparently, they're taking the medicines to that location in Alpha Central. Then, they move in shipments to a secured top-secret location somewhere else in the city. The shipments are moving through the night. Too risky to move in the day. Maybe if you catch them at the right time, they'll lead you straight to Kane.'

Having listened closely to Wayne, Jade did not notice until it was too late a familiar sound of a click from a gun very close near her right ear. The barrel of the gun now moved, touching the back of her head. Jade could do nothing but look ahead at Wayne who sat more comfortably now, with a smile rising on his face. His demeanour suddenly now calmer and more relaxed.

As it dawned on Jade that one of Wayne's guards had entered the office without her noticing, a sense of disappointment came over Jade of what her opinion now was of Wayne.

'Before you go off and do your job,' Wayne said, 'I'm going to have my own fun with you Jade.'

'Oh, Wayne,' Jade replied. 'You can't help but still think

with your dick.'

'I know I owe you for what you did. But that's one debt I want rid of. Strip naked now, Jade.'

Always comes down to the same thing with you, Wayne, Jade thought.

With her back to the guard pointing the gun, Jade remained calm and composed. 'I take it you're insured with this place?' Jade asked.

'Of course. You're thinking of standing up to my guard and making a mess of my office?'

'No. More like your guard making a shattering guest appearance on stage.'

Briefly, Wayne's look turned more concerned.

Before he could think a second longer, Jade gestured a move with her right arm and hand.

Unknown to Wayne and the guard, Jade had a mechanism strapped to her arm hidden on the inside sleeve of her coat. Attached to the mechanism was a hidden knife. Her moving gesture triggered the knife to slide down her arm into the palm of her hand. Letting her now grip the knife tight and in sight.

Jade wasted no time. Spinning so fast that the guard had no time to respond. Turning around one hundred and eighty degrees. Stabbing the knife into the guard's hand holding the gun. The guard screamed out in pain. Wayne looked on in shock. The pain from the knife forced the guard to lose grip of the gun. Letting the gun start to fall down to the floor.

Jade, alert and ready, lowered down to grab the guards' gun before it touched the floor. Catching it in mid-air. Rising to stand up straight, she aimed the gun and fired several shots into the large glass window overlooking the club. Bullet holes now spread in several spaces across the glass. The window began to crack but remained standing.

Jade looked back at the guard. Gripping the knife, she

stabbed through his hand. She quickly yanked the knife out of his wounded hand. Causing the guard to scream out in pain once again. To shut him up, Jade punched him in the face several times before finishing him off by kicking him hard in his groin.

Jade could see by the expression on his face that he properly felt the last one.

Jade then grabbed his suit tight in her hands. Taking one last look at his weak and painful face. 'You know, I do love a cracked glass wall. It's always so tempting,' Jade said.

Jade then threw the guard towards the gun-shot cracked large window. Instantly making the whole glass wall shatter.

The guard fell down to the floor in the main area of the club. Broken glass scattered all over his suit and surrounding floor. Falling down on the main stage where the ladies would perform in the club.

The sight of the fallen guard caused the women to run from the stage. Making the men run from the club.

Jade looked out of the shattered glass hole. Looking out into the club. Hearing screams and panic. Jade had just sent her message what she thought of this place. And she was thrilled that people were taking notice of her impact.

Jade could hear the nervous quick breathing from Wayne, still sat behind his desk in the office. Turning her attention back towards him, she walked back to stand in front of the desk. Now, raising the guard's gun that she still held and pointing it at Wayne's head.

'Jade. Please. I'm sorry. I'm so sorry,' Wayne started to cry as he spoke.

Jade did not move. Letting herself observe for several seconds how pathetic and small Wayne now looked.

Then, she lowered down the gun. Placing it in her coat pocket. She leaned down, placing her hands on the desk. Jade did not look angry or furious, but her eyes told a very different story.

Shopping

- Soap
- Fish, deli or peas × 2
- Stuffing
- Baps
- Spices
-

182 – 'still alive'

184 ↓

189 secret passage

191 ↓

197

201 →

{ 153 ↓
  154 ↑

Medicines/hostages?.

156 – 8
' Quiet ≠silent'?!
    160

161 back × 4

164
165 ↓
167 Dr Patel.
168
179 ✗

Bibles
'St Pat's Church'
{ 15 × 2

'Wayne, take a good look at your guard. That would've been you. One day, it still could be. But what you know and hear, little man, still has its uses. Don't ever cross me again.'

Jade leant up straight. Taking one last look at Wayne. Then she turned and started to leave the office. Before doing so, Wayne took the courage to speak up and say one more word.

'Tekker.'

Jade stopped walking. That was the name that Eve mentioned in jail, she thought. She looked over her shoulder back towards Wayne. She was curious to hear more.

'What did you say?'

'The group called Tekker,' Wayne replied. 'They got me the money to buy this place. I was part of the group. Then, I chose to leave. I got sucked into that drug underworld. And that's where you found me. They got in contact with me recently. I thought they'd forgotten about me. They said I could be useful to them soon.'

'Useful for what?'

'I don't know. They didn't tell me. All they said was you'd be hearing from us again soon.'

'You'd better let me know when they do,' Jade said with a strong command.

'I promise, Jade,' replied Wayne.

He had nothing more to say. With their talk finished, Jade now stormed out of Wayne's office.

Remembering the address Wayne had written down, Jade knew her night was still young. Hoping the night still had many rewards left to find. Most notably leading her right to Jack Kane.

Chapter 29

The address on the note led Jade to a dark back street in the heart of Alpha Central. The night had turned to freezing temperatures. Cold rain began falling. Trickling down the side walls of the tall buildings. Pavements turned wet with puddles scattered far into the distance. Water overflowing from leaking drainage pipes up above causing heavy water splashes falling down to street level. Only two lamp post lights were on in this dark back street. It was quiet and silent. The only sound echoing loud on the street coming from the loud splashes made from the puddles and rain.

Then, breaking the sound, echoing down the long stretch of the street, was the cracking sound from Jade's heels making contact with the concrete ground.

Jade slowly walked down the empty street. She was alone with no one else present in her sight.

Her long, straight black hair began getting wet in the rain. Her face quickly became wet, too.

She looked up at the tall buildings on either side of her. She could not see anyone observing her from the rooftops. Moving on, she looked at the decor of the building to her right. She recognised the building. It was formerly a tall building used as a high street shop for one of the big retailers. Now, with the pressure on the high street, the retailer had closed down the shop and the building now stood derelict. Looking behind her, back towards the main road, Jade's attention was caught by a tram passing by on the track line running down the road. Having stopped at the Market Street tram stop, the tram had disturbed the silence on the back street. Now having moved on, Jade turned to look back ahead of her.

Jade looked along the wall of the derelict retail store. In front of her, she saw three metal delivery shutters closed shut. Moving slowly up to one of the shutters, Jade gently placed her ear on the metal.

She heard movement. Possibly chatter. Sound of objects or trolleys being moved along the floor. Convinced of activity taking place inside, Jade stepped back to look up at the high windows. Hoping to see anything or anyone. Then she saw it. Seeing the flicker of candlelight. The shadows of men moving in front of the light. Jade started walking down the back street, searching for a back door.

She made her way back down the end of the street she had come from. Leading her back towards the main road. Before reaching the road, she now noticed a closed door. Hidden inside a dark shadowed alcove. Approaching, Jade moved her hands around the edge of the door slowly. She could not find an easy way to enter. Frustration started to build up within her. Stepping back out into the street, her eye got attracted to look down at the far end by a pair of bright headlamps of a car moving down the street some distance away. The bright light shone towards her.

Instantly, Jade ducked back to hide within the door alcove. Hidden from view, Jade edged her eye around the edge of the alcove.

The car stopped moving. She saw it was placed in front of one of the closed metal delivery shutters. With the bright light from the headlamps shining down towards her end of the street, it was difficult to make out what was happening, if anything, beyond the light. Focusing her eyes, she saw a young, big, muscular man step out of the driver's seat side of the car, walking

161

up to one of the closed shutters and started banging his fist on the metal shutter three times. She then heard and could see the shutter slowly moving up. Once the shutter had cleared above the head of the muscular man, she saw him enter the building.

Jade knew this was her chance. She moved out of the alcove. Making her way towards the open delivery entrance. Quietly reaching the entrance, she pressed her body as much towards the outer wall as to remain unseen from anyone within the building. She remained silent and slow in her movement.

The nearer she reached the open shutter, the more she heard the sound of a conversation between the muscular man and the workers already within the building.

Now reaching the shutter, Jade cautiously peered into the delivery area of the building.

She saw two trucks being stocked full of medical equipment. Workers nearby placed them in boxes and crates. Jade could now clearly see the muscular man talking to the workers. It was Tyson, Jack Kane's right-hand man. She could hear clearly now Tyson's demands that all the stock must be moved tonight and that the next journey to the secret location would be the last one.

With no time to lose, Jade got out her mobile phone. She took a photo of the licence plate of Tyson's car. Without being seen, Jade moved into the delivery area. Staying as close to the wall so as not to be seen. She lowered herself down, hiding behind several crates.

Carefully lifting her head above the crate, she aimed the camera on her phone to take snapshots of all the important details taking place where she was. Shots like Tyson directing the workers, workers moving equipment into the boxes and crates, the crates and boxes being placed into the trucks and finally, Tyson paying off the workers.

Ducking back under cover, Jade attached all the photos to a

text message. Typing out the message, it read 'TRACK MY PHONE. FOLLOW MY SIGNAL'. Pressing send, she sent the message to the two men she trusted most. Louis and Tanner.

She knew that once Louis had this message, he now had the proof to show Julius. Evidence to give just cause for the police to find and arrest Jack Kane and his associates for stealing vital medical supplies. All Jade needed now was the knowledge of where Kane kept the kidnapped children.

With no time to lose, Jade began approaching one of the delivery trucks. Staying as low to the ground to remain hidden. Jade remained unseen, below and between the boxes and crates.

But Jade was now in trouble. With all shipments beginning to be placed in the trucks, her hidden route would not remain hidden for much longer.

Noticing Tyson and the workers focused on the supplies on the truck furthest away from Jade, she took her chance to reach the open back of the truck nearest to her.

She hopped up silently into the back of the truck, moving as far back inside the truck as she could.

Several boxes were already placed inside. Covered over by several large plastic garments.

Jade lowered down, covering herself under the garment on the side of the box nearest the driver's end of the truck.

Several minutes later, all the shipments had filled up all the space available in both trucks.

With Tyson giving one last look of the delivery area of the building, now being empty of stock, he was content all the supplies were now stored on the two trucks.

Tyson gave his command for the workers to get in the trucks and follow Tyson in his car to the secret location.

Jade sat still undercover. Hearing the banging and shutting of doors, along with typical small men's talk, Jade heard the engine being switched on.

She did not hear anybody get into the back of the truck. She was secure in knowing she was alone.

Feeling the truck was now moving, Jade stepped out of hiding. Looking out the open back of the truck.

Losing her balance slightly, Jade gripped hold of the garment that was covering several boxes to keep her balance. Looking out the back, she could see the delivery area of the old retail building moving further away far in the distance.

With no way to see into the front of the truck, Jade's mind had to think backwards as to where they were going, based on looking at the nearby surroundings through the open back of the truck.

*

Minutes later, Jade noticed the surroundings. The truck was moving into the eastern part of the city. The main road was quiet and empty with no other vehicles in sight.

Feeling the truck was beginning to slow down, Jade began to get ready to go under the garment for cover. Yet she was curious to know where the drop-off point was going to be.

The truck slowed to a stop. Waiting for a security check at the entrance to a site. Jade could see a sign nearby reading 'NEW SMITHFIELD MARKET'. A site Jade knew was formerly a trade and marketplace. A secret site now being used as a vital point of Jack Kane's business empire.

Jade was ready and about to step into Jack Kane's secret domain.

Chapter 30

A worker was alone. Carrying out boxes one by one from the delivery truck. The delivery floor area of the Smithfield Market warehouse was level with the truck. Now reaching the boxes near the back of the truck, the worker uncovered the garment covering them. To his surprise, a very attractive young woman with long, wet black hair sat on the floor of the truck, looking up at him.

Before he could think another thought, the attractive woman leapt up. Instantly punching him in the face very hard. Falling unconscious, the worker fell to the ground of the truck.

*

Jade placed the garment over the worker's unconscious body.

Getting out her gun, Jade checked that all the barrels were full. Satisfied, Jade made her way out of the truck.

The rain had now stopped. Looking left and right at the delivery area, Jade saw she was alone. A few feet away, Jade heard activity coming from behind a closed metal doorway.

Calmly, she walked up to the door. Gently holding the door handle, she quietly opened the door enough to see inside.

Looking on, inside the warehouse, she could see the workers removing supplies from the delivered boxes and crates. At the far end, she saw doctors, scientists and technicians standing near the entrance to a lab door.

Jade wanted to know more about what they were doing.

165

Looking up, she suddenly noticed a high metal walkway going all around the edge of the walls of the large warehouse. Noticing a closed fire exit door on that level, Jade knew she had found a possible way into the warehouse.

Closing the door, she stepped back. Starting to walk her way round the exterior of the warehouse.

She reached a metal fire escape. With the ladder placed in a high horizontal level, Jade ran up, jumping up high to get grip of the ladder. After several attempts, she finally got hold of a step on the ladder. Forcing the ladder down into a vertical position. Climbing the ladder up onto a metal staircase, Jade pulled the ladder back up into its horizontal position.

Now, Jade was free to climb up the exterior fire staircase. Reaching the top, she faced a closed metal fire escape door. Readying her gun, Jade slowly moved the door open. As she hoped, the door led onto the high metal walkway inside the warehouse. Once inside, Jade instantly lowered down so as not to be seen by the many male workers below.

Looking below her, Jade now saw more clearly what she saw earlier. Boxes and crates of drugs, medicines, chemicals. Each was taken out and moved into nearby labs by the doctors.

Jade was standing directly above the end of the warehouse near the labs. She scanned her eyes over the whole area of the warehouse.

Then, she saw him. Jack Kane with Tyson standing by his side. Kane was shaking hands with a scientist who appeared to be the leader of the group of scientists.

They now started walking. Moved to stand directly beneath Jade on the metal walkway. Now closer to her, Jade could make out more of their conversation.

'Sir, you now have the city's medical supplies stocked under one roof,' the head scientist said. He was a small man and was of Indian descent. His name was Doctor Patel. 'With this much, you can now trade with the health service at the prices you now set.'

'Or hold them to ransom,' replied Kane.

'Yes, sir,' Doctor Patel replied. 'Rest assured, with all these supplies, you are secured in your position for the next ten years.'

Kane felt disappointed in that comment.

'It's not enough,' Kane said. 'Ten years is not enough. I want enough security for twenty years, thirty years, forty. Until the day I die. I want to make a permanent statement. I'm not here to have power for a short term in office.'

'But, sir, with our staff, we're stretched already as it is,' Patel replied.

'Really? Well, maybe I'll get your boss on the phone and see if we can hire a few more people. Tyson, call the doctor's boss.'

Tyson got out his mobile and called the number that had been provided to him. The scientist was now looking more nervous.

'Is something wrong?' Kane asked Doctor Patel.

'You don't know what type of person my boss is, Mister Kane.'

Having made the call, Tyson walked back towards Kane, ready to hand the phone over. 'Sir,' Tyson said looking shocked.

'Who is it?' Kane said looking puzzled.

'New Dawn,' replied Tyson.

Kane was both shocked and amazed. Then he turned to look back at Patel. 'You work for New Dawn?' Kane asked.

'Yes,' replied Patel. 'You wanted help. So, they allowed me to help you.'

Giving no reply, Kane looked back at Tyson. Taking the phone from him, Kane walked a few paces away to be by himself to take the call.

Above on the walkway, Jade observed Kane in his conversation. But she could not hear what was being said. From her vantage point, Kane had his back to her. The conversation on the phone remained private and secret.

Kane finished the call. Turning back to face both Tyson and Patel, Kane had a big smile on his face.

'Your boss has agreed with me,' Kane said towards Doctor Patel. 'More of your science friends will soon be on their way. Go get ready for them.'

'Yes, sir,' Patel answered.

With Kane now alone with Tyson, Kane now changed topic. 'Are all the children I wanted been captured?' Kane asked.

Jade, now more interested, lowered her ear down closer to the metal floor of the walkway. 'Yes, sir,' replied Tyson. 'They're at a secured location outside the city.'

'Where? I want to see them,' Kane demanded.

'The last place someone like Tanner wouldn't dare go to,' Tyson said. Jade looked puzzled but curious to know what Tyson meant by that.

Suddenly, Jade heard the familiar sound of a loud click of a gun barrel touching the side temple of her head. A worker had found her along the walkway.

I really need to sharpen my hearing to when someone is creeping up behind me, Jade thought.

Prison has made Jade be a little rusty.

'Don't you dare say anything,' the worker commanded. 'Stand up and give me your gun.' She did so. As she rose to stand up, the worker kept his gun touching her head.

'Hey, boss!' the worker shouted out. Kane and Tyson looked

168

up above at the walkway. 'Look at the sexy babe I caught listening in. Now I'm ready to shove my gun right through her.' The worker laughed. The other workers laughed along, too. Jade was not amused by the sexual innuendo of the joke.

'That will have to wait!' Kane shouted out. The workers all stopped laughing. 'Bring her down here.'

As the worker escorted Jade along the walkway, down a metal staircase to ground level, Kane stayed focused. Not taking his eyes off Jade. The closer Jade got to Kane, the more he noticed the anger and rage hidden behind those eyes of hers.

For Jade, she now stood in front of the man who ordered her son Sean to be killed. If it was not for Tyson, the workers and scientists that encircled her and Kane, Jade would love to do nothing more than give Kane what he deserved most. But with the workers outnumbering her, looking Jade up and down with a sexual, voyeuristic stare, Jade knew the wrong move could provoke them to take advantage of her. She knew she had to remain calm. The wrong move now would just make things worse.

With everyone silent, Kane walked slowly up to Jade to stand in front of her. The two looked at the other eye to eye for the very first time.

'So, you're, Jade Hall. I've always wanted to meet you,' Kane said calmly.

'Feelings mutual,' Jade replied.

'Do you like what you see here?' Kane asked gesturing towards the medical stock all supplied in the warehouse and labs.

'I see you're a real true addict,' replied Jade. 'You lust for profit, power and greed. You don't care who you hurt on your way up the career ladder. You want to hold the city to ransom so you can get what you want? You're just a mad nutcase who looks good in a suit. That's all you've got going for you.'

'A madman in a suit?' Kane asked. 'Is that what you think? It's this city and the system that's mad and in chaos. My motto is, where there's chaos, there's opportunity. I'm smart enough to take a chance from all the chaos. Even from the chaos I create. And now you're here, it's all come full circle.'

'What you talking about? Full circle?' Jade asked.

'You really don't know?' Kane quietly asked.

Just then, Kane looked up close at Jade's face. Staring deep into her eyes. 'Let me tell you a little story, Jade.'

Chapter 31

It was the night everything changed. But Peter Hall didn't know it yet.

After all, he was busy at work in his study in his city centre flat on Whitworth Street.

Peter Hall sat working on his laptop in his office at his Alpha Central flat. An upmarket venue for one as important as he. He was finishing up the last of his personal dealings before focusing on the busy days that lay ahead of him.

Now in his mid-thirties, he aspired to be a leading political figure for the City of Alpha. Beginning with his campaign to be the next elected Mayor of Alpha City.

He knew his journey ahead would not be smooth or easy. Typing away on his laptop, dealing with a personal document he was finishing off, he gave a brief glimpse of the several newspapers scattered on his desk beside him, with headlines reading various titles of revolt, riots, and gang warfare taking place on the outskirts of the city centre limits.

At this time, nothing could stop the oncoming storm of riots, troubles and gangs escalating further within the city boundaries. And Peter knew the type of people who would be leading those gangs in their crusade.

For all the powers the police had at their disposal, nothing could stop this threat to the city. Rising more and more as the years went by.

Peter knew the time had come to act. Either now or never to

save the city from this downfall. He believed he could change the tide and bring this city back from the brink of collapse. Supported by his wife Jane, he believed he could make a difference for the people and for the city.

But first things first. This document he was typing up. He was working on a declaration that made a personal piece of business final and done with. A regretful chapter of his past. One he was finally able to draw a line in the sand with and move on in his life. He had not wanted it to come to this. Even his feelings of sadness overwhelmed him as he typed away on the keyboard. But this was it. The day to look forward and never look back. This was a new beginning for Peter and his family.

Once he had finished typing, he sat back in his chair, staring at the laptop screen. Looking over the document and the words typed up within. All he had to do was click and send. Hesitating, he slowly moved to sit back up straight. Moving his mouse, he clicked 'Send'. Then, a blank screen.

It was over. Finally.

Shaking off the thought of what he had just done, Peter turned his focus to his upcoming campaign. Thinking of the days and weeks ahead of going all over the region and meeting the voters, local people, and businesses. Planning for his speeches at the local rallies. Then came the darkest thought at the back of his mind. He knew he would be an enemy and become a target. It was all a matter of when will his new enemies show their faces.

*

A young Jack Kane sat quietly and calmly in the back of a black limousine car. Dressed neat, clean, business-like and slim build. Wearing a black suit, black tie that blended well with his gelled-back black hair. He was a man with a mission. And it would start tonight.

At the driver's seat sat a young Tyson. Silent and focused on driving his boss through the city centre, he waited patiently for Kane's next command.

Tonight, the city centre streets were quiet and empty as Tyson drove deeper into the heart of the city. The lamppost lights shone and moved through the car as they passed them. From Kane's seat, he saw the headlamps of the vehicle behind them. Its lights reflected back into Tyson's inner rear-view mirror. There was no need for Kane to question who was in the vehicle behind. He knew it was a black van carrying ten men who all worked for him. All armed men carrying knives and guns. They were Kane's gang. And tonight, he had set them a very special task.

'Slow down, Tyson,' Kane commanded as he looked up ahead of them.

'Are you sure, sir?' Tyson asked cautiously.

'I'm sure. I was told this is where I'd find him.'

Tyson started slowing down the car. He picked up his radio that was placed on the seat beside him and spoke into it.

'OK, slow the van down. We're here.'

Tyson pulled the car up outside the entrance on Whitworth Street to a block of city centre flats. Stepping out of the car, he ran round to Kane's side of the car to open his boss' door. As he did, the black van pulled up behind them. The group of armed men jumped out of the back of the van. Quickly moving to stand in one line to attention on the pavement.

Kane stood still, looking at his men as he stepped out of the car. Tyson leant into the car and grabbed Kane's coat. Having it ready, Tyson slid Kane's long black coat onto him. Once his coat was on, Kane gave a thankful smile to Tyson. With that, Kane gestured with his head for Tyson to move to stand in line. As Tyson walked away, Kane took his first look up at the multi-storey building. Kane looked back at his men, ready to address them.

'Now then. When we get in, you know what to do. And you know who we want. It's time for the fear to run wild. Go.'

Just then, the men turned away and started running through the entrance of the building. Both Tyson and Kane stood back, watching them. Leaving Kane and Tyson alone on the night street. 'This is it, boss,' Tyson said. 'Once we've got him, nothing will be the same again.'

Kane gave no reply. He did not even look at Tyson. His focus was to look up at the building. The moment he had planned for such a long time was about to begin.

*

Jane Hall walked up to her husband in his study. Holding their baby daughter Jade in her arms.

She saw him walking in a circle, holding sheets of paper, reading them over and over again. He appeared to be speaking out aloud his speech that he would be giving in the morning.

At this late hour, he was still going over it. Making sure it sounded right. Knowing she would support him through thick and thin, she knew this was her chance to have her moment alone with her husband, whom she loved so deeply.

Walking up to Peter, she placed her hand gently on his shoulder, which slowly stopped him from walking around the room.

'Peter, enough. You've done enough work today.'

As she said that, Peter stopped walking and looked right into her eyes.

'I'm sorry,' Peter replied. 'With this speech tomorrow, I just want to make sure I've got all my policies down and precise.'

Jane moved around to stand right in front of Peter and kissed him gently. Moving back, she looked deep into his eyes, which were full of love in her heart.

'It can wait,' she said. 'It will all still be here tomorrow for you. Come to bed, Peter.'

At that moment, Peter threw the sheets of paper down on his desk. Then, looking back at both Jane and their daughter Jade, a sense of calm and peace came over him, looking at the two females who were the love of his life.

Giving his own gentle kiss to Jane, he smiled. 'I truly love you, Jane. With all my heart.'

'I love you too. My husband,' Jane replied, full of warmth and love.

Then, both Jane and Peter looked at their baby daughter Jade. Feeling happy and content at now having their own family.

'And here's our little miracle that our love rewarded us with,' Peter said as he gently caressed Jade's baby head. Smiling at her as he did.

But then, the peace of their moment was broken.

The gunshot fires from floors below were heard by both of them. The echoes of screams and shouts from people could be heard.

Both Peter and Jane were concerned to know what was going on beneath them.

'What was that?' Jane asked nervously.

The gunfire continued. They were slowly getting louder and louder from where Peter and Jane could hear them.

Both their pulses and heart rates were getting faster and faster.

Peter began to trust his instincts. There was a strong chance he knew who those gunmen were coming for. And he was not going to take any chances. He had to act fast and quickly.

'Jane, listen to me. Go to the bedroom. Take Jade. Lock the door. Keep quiet. And don't say anything.'

'What about you?'

'Jane, please. Just go.'

With time being short, Peter gently kissed his daughter's head.

The gunfire outside was now so loud. Jane had no choice. She gave Peter one last glance and then quickly ran into the bedroom holding Jade. Peter watched Jane go into the bedroom at the end of the long corridor. Seeing her shut the door, he could hear Jane turning the key in the lock on her side.

With no time to lose, Peter walked back into his study. Walking towards a large picture frame on the wall, he took it down from where it hung. Behind where the frame was placed was his own safe. He started to undo the code on the safe. But time was running out. He had to remain calm to remember the code combination. Meanwhile, the gunshots fired were now sounding even louder. Nearly reaching the door to his flat.

*

In the bedroom, Jane had been quickly moving away blankets, sheets and bedding from the inside floor of their wardrobe. Wrapping Jade up in a small blanket, Jane gently kissed Jade on the cheek. A tear fell down Jane's cheek. Then Jane placed her daughter down on the floor of the wardrobe as far back as she could go. Then she started placing back the sheets and bedding to cover over and hide her baby daughter Jade.

'I love you,' Jane quietly said almost crying.

Moving back, she closed the large wardrobe doors. Then she moved towards the bedroom windows. The furthest place away from the bedroom door. Fear and panic started building up inside her. Her heart is now racing faster than ever.

Please, God, she thought, *don't let them search the wardrobe.*

*

Peter had unlocked the safe. Opening it, he took out his loaded gun from inside. With no time left, he walked towards his open office door. Peering around the edge of the doorway. Looking down the long corridor of the flat towards the main door that was between him and the bedroom.

Now, the silence was heard. The first time, it was heard in minutes. All Peter could hear for this brief moment was the sound of his breath and the heavy, fast beat of his heart.

Any second, he thought. *Any moment now.*

BANG! BANG! BANG!

The bullets smashed loudly on the flat door like shattering glass into a thousand pieces. The door had dozens of holes, with light from outside shining through each one. Peter saw the door being pushed inward. Feet hitting and pushing it hard. Making it collapse finally on the floor. The gunmen could now make their way into the flat.

Peter saw the first two gunmen make their way through the opening. He pointed his gun. Shot both gunmen down instantly. The force of the bullets made them fall back into the building corridor. Collapsed and dead.

Suddenly, two more came into view. They also were trying to get through the open doorway. But Peter was quicker than them. Shooting them both, they were down for the count, collapsing dead in the open doorway.

And now, silence once again.

After a few seconds, Peter cautiously began walking up towards the open doorway to the flat. Still pointing his gun forward. Peering round the doorway out into the building corridor, he saw the fallen gunmen's corpses.

Then, another gunman jumped out from hiding in front of him. Shooting towards Peter but missing him. No time to think. Peter shot the gunman down at close range.

BANG!

A gunshot hit Peter from the opposite direction. Opposite where the gunman he had just shot came from. Shooting him in the back.

The force of the bullet made Peter collapse, leaning on the door frame helplessly. Turning to look behind him at the other end of the building corridor, he could see Tyson standing at the far end, pointing his gun at him.

Peter, now weak from the wound, struggled to lift up his gun. He was too late. Tyson now shot Peter again. This time in the chest. The blood from the wounds was now soaking up on Peter's clothes. Peter, going into shock, fell back away from the doorway. Collapsing back into the corridor of the flat. As he crashed down on the floor, the gun slipped out of his grip. Sliding across the floor.

Peter could hear Tyson's footsteps walking up towards the open doorway. He glimpsed in half a daze at the closed bedroom door.

Oh God, Peter thought.

Tyson now stood above the wounded, bleeding Peter. Placing his gun in his pocket, he moved to stand directly above Peter. Tyson picked him up. Dragging him back into his study. The blood from the wounds now made a small trail of blood behind Peter. Once in the middle of the office, Tyson dropped Peter's body down hard on the floor. Lying on top of the carpet. Tyson stood intent to stand above Peter's wounded body.

Lying there helpless, Peter could hear the slow echo of footsteps out in the hallway. Making their way slowly up towards the open study door. Turning his eyes up, Peter saw the sight of Jack Kane smiling, looking confident. Slowly, Kane walked towards Peter. Panning his eyes up and down Peter's body. Paying close attention to the wounds in the chest and back. Then, having looked at the body, Kane now focused his attention on looking at Peter right into his eyes.

'The secret to how the battle is won, Peter,' Kane said, 'is not to attack with all your soldiers all at once. But to strike first, wear your enemy down and then strike again. Strike down the symbols of hope, and you give rise to chaos and fear. And where there's chaos, there's opportunity. And you know all about opportunity, don't you, Peter?'

'Whatever you're after, people will fight against you, Kane.'

'Until people's hearts break completely. And what can break their heart more than striking down the light of hope for the people of this city? That hope being you.'

'If I give them hope, what the hell do you give them?'

'I don't give, Peter. I take, even from someone like you. Tyson, search the flat.'

With that command, Tyson left the room. Seeing him leave,

Peter tried to lift himself up off the floor. But still too weak, he knew it was too late.

Kane placed his foot down on Peter. Preventing him from moving. To add insult, Kane moved his foot onto the wound on Peter's chest. Causing a shockwave of pain to go through Peter's body.

Peter started to hear Jane scream. *No, please, no,* he thought.

Tyson carried Jane into the office. Throwing her on the floor. Once she saw Peter on the floor, her tears began to take over. Falling down her face. She quickly tried to move towards Peter. But Tyson grabbed her arm. Making her stop moving. Tyson was not letting go. His grip stayed tight and strong.

Kane looked over at Jane. Moved his foot off Peter's chest. He could see how emotional and distressed she was. Walking towards her, he looked her in the eye.

'Do you love this man?' Kane asked quietly. Jane gave no reply.

Then, Kane looked back over at Peter. As he did, he placed his right hand in his coat pocket.

'You know, you're right, Peter,' Kane said. 'You do give hope. And while there's hope, there's life.'

Instantly, out of his right pocket, Kane held a gun. Pointing it at Jane. He shot directly into her head.

BANG!

Jane's corpse collapsed dead on the floor. 'NO!' shouted Peter. 'No. No.'

He started to cry. He looked on helplessly at his wife's dead body. Hopelessly, he started crawling along the floor towards his wife's corpse with tears in his eyes. Then, he heard above him a click in Kane's gun trigger. Peter looked back up at Kane. Seeing Kane aiming his gun at his head.

'And while there's life, Peter,' Kane said, 'there's me. Jack Kane to choke it out.' *BANG*!

Kane shot Peter in the head. His dead body fell back on the floor. Blood now pouring out of his head. Beginning to soak into the carpet. Thinking nothing of what he had just done, Kane gave an order to Tyson.

'See if anybody else is in the flat. And kill them.'

'Yes, sir,' Tyson replied.

Tyson left Kane to look down at Peter and Jane's bodies, knowing the plan had worked. The murder had happened. And the moment he had wanted was about to begin.

*

In the bedroom, Tyson walked in slowly. Looking around the whole room with a gun in hand. Looking under the bed. No one was there. He stood back up.

Then, his eyes caught sight of the closed wardrobe door.

Pointing his gun at the door, he walked towards it. He opened it wide. Inside, there were clothes and coats hanging up along the wall. Along the floor were sheets, bedding and blankets neatly stacked alongside each other. With no one there, Tyson closed the wardrobe door and left the bedroom. Leaving to look in the other remaining rooms in the flat.

*

Minutes later, Tyson met up with Kane in the corridor outside the flat.

'Well?' Kane asked.

'There's no one else there. It was just those two,' Tyson

replied.

'Good. It's time to get the ball rolling. Time for my gang to raise hell over the city. Pick up the men's dead bodies. We'll dump them in the canals.'

The other armed gunmen, still alive, picked up the dead gunmen's corpses. With that command, Kane, and Tyson, along with the rest of the armed gunmen still alive, started to leave the floor of the building. Kane's night had been a success.

Except.

*

Back in the flat, in the bedroom wardrobe, still hidden under the sheets and blankets at the far end, was Peter and Jane's most precious treasured thing in the whole world. Their baby daughter, Jade.

No more than six months old, Jade was quiet and still and yet she started to cry. Even covered and hidden from view could not stop the little baby Jade from hearing the screams of her mother being dragged and taken away to her death. Also, hearing the two gunshots that killed her parents.

For Jade, those screams and gunshots were already beginning to sit deep within her. The sounds that would stay with her. Haunting her for the many, many years to come.

That was the night everything changed. But Jade Hall didn't know it yet.

Only that a new path in her life had now been forced upon her. The beginning of her scarred journey.

Chapter 32

'You bastard. You're the one who scarred my life from the start,' Jade said full of shock from hearing the story.

Kane took out his gun from his coat pocket. Staring at it proudly. Then he looked deep into Jade's eyes.

'You have your father's eyes,' Kane said. 'I remember seeing his eyes whilst I pointed this gun right at his head. Then, seeing him so scared, I blew his brains out with this gun.'

Jade stood frozen in that moment. Hearing those words echo in her mind.

Jade's heart sank from this revelation. She was in the presence of her parents' murderer. The event that shaped Jade's life. Making Jade grow up an orphan.

'You killed my parents.'

'I killed hope. I killed a born leader. The competition. Your father and I were very much alike. He was running for office. When the city was crumbling around his feet, he grabbed the opportunity to take control of power over the city.'

'My father was giving hope. All you gave was greed and a dictatorship in a suit. It disguises the psychopath you really are. It's all about image over substance with you. Deep down, I know what you are. When it all comes down to who you really are inside, you've revealed how hollow, shallow and unfulfilled a pathetic man you truly are. In the end, what it all boils down to is that Jack Kane is one truly dark, twisted prick.'

Kane stared at Jade. He gave no reply. Then he gave a click

with his fingers. Instantly, Tyson stomped up to Jade.

And then *WHACK*! Tyson punched Jade hard in the face. Forcing her to fall down to the floor. The group of workers circling started laughing at Jade. Kane casually looked at them in approval.

Then, looking down at her, he saw her bruised face looking up in defiance of him.

'All those words,' Kane said. 'When a man has all the power, there's no place for a woman to have an opinion.'

Just then, Tyson ran up and kicked Jade hard in the stomach. She truly felt the pain from the hit.

She rolled onto her other side, away from Tyson. Again, the workers looked down laughing at the pitiful state of Jade.

'You're a woman who needs to be taught a lesson. A woman who needs to be shown her place?' Kane said in a calm manner.

Tyson grabbed the collar of Jade's long black coat. Forcing her body to lift up off the ground.

With his free hand, Tyson punched Jade hard in the face again. Letting go of the collar, Tyson let her body collapse down to the floor. Lying on her back, looking up. Her face was now cut, bruised and bleeding.

'You see, Jade, a woman must be held down by the man for the good of himself, his ambitions and society. And when he needs her, she needs to stand by her man as well,' Kane confidently said.

Tyson took the chance to hit Jade hard in her ribs. She could feel the pain but refused to scream out.

'Women are nothing more than a status symbol for the man,' Kane continued. 'But the truth is, they're only beautiful on the surface. They're the ones who are the shallow, hollow opportunists underneath. All they care about is wealth, the latest fashion trends, and celebrity fame. Men have the strength and the power. Women are just a trophy for a man's life. And in the end, the world sees women the way men want women to be seen.'

As she stared up at Kane speak whilst still lying on the floor, Jade's thoughts now became crystal clear where she stood.

So, it's all come down to this, Jade thought. *I am a woman fighting for my identity in a man's world.*

Finishing his speech, the group of workers laughed and applauded Kane, giving their support of his views. Meanwhile, Jade full of pain, cuts and bruises slowly picked herself up off the floor. Standing defiantly in front of all these men. Not expressing any of the pain she was now feeling.

'You see, Jade, I have that power. And I have the power to make or break you,' Kane said.

'You know what people like you have a problem with?' Jade asked as she spat some blood out of her mouth.

'Tell me,' Kane said mockingly.

'You are smart. But not smart enough.'

'How so?'

'You're smart enough to take on the system. But not smart enough to beat it at its own game.'

'And how did you figure that out?'

Jade placed her hand in her coat pocket. Taking out her mobile phone, she showed it for everyone to see.

'Because the police were tracking my phone,' Jade said. 'Right to this warehouse. All that talk and letting you beat me up was just a way to stall your attention away from the big picture. And when they storm in here seeing you with all these supplies, one word will come to mind that sums up your situation, Kane. Busted.'

Kane then turned, looking up at the large warehouse windows. The colours of police headlights shine all around outside. The sound of police sirens swarming the exterior.

The workers and scientists' mood drastically turned to worry and concern. Tyson also started to become tense and anxious at the situation.

Looking back at Jade, Kane saw her now looking confident and sure of herself. Now feeling frustrated and angry, Kane's attitude turned to rage.

'You bitch!' Kane shouted out.

'That's right. The bitch, the daughter, the mother. Jade Hall is my name.'

Chapter 33

'Jack Kane! This is the police!' Louis Walker shouted into the megaphone he was holding.

Police cars and vans surrounded the exterior of the warehouse. Police and armed officers were all ready to storm the building.

Louis stood beside Julius, waiting for the command to enter the warehouse. Julius stood still whilst Louis continued speaking into the megaphone.

'You're all under arrest for drug smuggling, child kidnapping and breach of the Alpha Central treaty! You all have sixty seconds to step out of the building, or we will raid the building armed and in numbers!'

*

Inside the warehouse, Kane and Tyson heard the message loud and clear. With concern rising, Tyson walked towards Kane.

'Sir, what can we do? They'll catch us red-handed in here.'

'I know. I know,' Kane replied.

'Do we strike back?'

'Get the men ready.'

At that point, Tyson walked towards the workmen and members of Kane's gang. He passed on the order. All of the group ran off in different directions. Getting themselves armed and ready to fight back.

Meanwhile, Kane stared back at Jade. Now raising his gun, he pointed it in fury at Jade.

'So, you told them where to find me. Bad call for you. Now, it's time for some poetic justice. Father, mother, and daughter. All killed with the same gun.'

Kane was ready to pull the trigger. Then, Kane heard a loud bang overhead. Both he and Jade looked up.

Up on the high metal stairway, the fire exit door Jade had entered the warehouse through slammed open.

Stepping onto the high walkway with a gun in hand stood Tanner.

Jade felt relief to see her friend. Kane realised that Tanner had not yet seen him. Tanner's attention was focused on the workmen and Kane's henchmen, who were all armed and ready.

Kane took his chance. Moving his guns aim away from Jade and pointing it up to shoot Tanner.

Now Jade had her chance. With Kane distracted, Jade ran up to Kane as hard as she could. Rugby tackling him down to the ground.

Kane, losing his balance, made his gun go off by accident. Shooting up but towards the metal stairway a few feet away from Tanner.

Hearing the nearby gunshot echo throughout the warehouse, Tanner saw the sudden turn of the workers and henchmen, all now looking up at him. Tanner knew he was now in trouble. Seeing them begin to raise their guns and armour, aiming up towards him on the walkway, Tanner wasted no time. He started shooting down the men on the ground.

In mere seconds, the blast of noise of gunfight echoed loudly, enveloping the whole warehouse.

Outside, Julius, Louis and the other officers could now clearly hear the loud burst of gunfire taking place within the warehouse.

Julius knew this was the time to strike and shouted out the command.

'OK. LET'S GO. NOW. NOW.'

Instantly, all armed police officers stormed the warehouse by the main entrance. Both Julius and Louis entered armed and ready.

*

Inside, Jade lay on top of Kane. Kicking his gun out of his hand. Making it slide along the floor several feet out of his reach.

Jade took her chance to start punching the hell out of Kane's face. Hitting him hard so his face turned bruised purple and bloody red. Giving every punch, every hit with full passion. Giving all she had to give for her, her parents, and her son.

But then she was stopped by a hard punch to her jaw by Tyson, who stood above her. The force of the punch forced Jade off Kane. Making her fall to the floor.

Tyson took the chance to help Kane up off the floor.

'Sir,' Tyson said. 'You'd better go. Get out of here while you can. I'll take care of her. Take the secret passage. Hide where nobody will find you.'

Kane gave no reply. With an understanding look, Kane walked away from Tyson and left the warehouse unseen.

With his boss safely away, Tyson turned his attention back to Jade, who was dazed and slowly picking herself up off the floor.

'Now I'll finish what I started with you,' Tyson said.

'I'm waiting for you. You dick.' Jade readied her stance, which was similar to that of a boxer.

Ready and prepared, Tyson stormed up to Jade and both started fighting and beating the hell out of the other.

*

Up above on the metal walkway, Tanner was running out of bullets and cover. He was in danger of having nothing left to defend himself with.

Taking a chance to see where everyone was, he could see Jade fighting Tyson. He could not see Kane anywhere. But he caught glimpse of a dozen or so scientists taking their chance to escape the warehouse by a back door. All being led and ordered by Doctor Patel. Escaping the carnage of the battle that was beginning to ensue.

*

Julius and Louis had entered a long corridor running adjacent to the interior warehouse. Looking for a way in, Julius and Louis, followed by armed officers, stopped by a closed door.

Hearing the gun fighting coming loudest from behind this door, Julius took his chance and kicked down the door. Inside, none of the workers could hear the door banging open due to the loud gunfire.

Looking through the open doorway, Julius could see Tyson fighting Jade at the far end of the warehouse.

Julius then had a thought. An opportunity. A personal motive clouded his thoughts. This was his chance to get rid of Kane and his gang. Taking them out of the picture could cover over his corrupt dealings with Kane in the past.

And Jade. Someone he had never trusted. Someone he knew was a threat to uncovering his dirty past. This chance was too good to let go of.

Unbeknownst to Julius, Louis, too, had spotted Jade. Louis could see the open boxes and crates of all the medical supplies that had been stolen.

Julius paid no attention to that. His focus was on Kane and Jade. 'There's too many of them,' Julius said. 'We'll have to risk it.'

Louis saw Julius get out a grenade. Julius was ready to throw it in the direction of Jade and Tyson.

But Louis, not aware of that, became concerned for both Jade and the destruction of the medical supplies.

'Sir, wait,' Louis said. 'It's too risky. We can't risk destroying the stock. The city needs it; everyone, follow my lead.'

Louis entered the warehouse, followed by the group of armed officers. Julius stood still by the doorway, letting all the officers pass him by.

Inside the warehouse, a large gunfight started between the police and Kane's henchmen. Each hid for cover behind the crates and boxes scattered over the large warehouse.

Up above on the metal stairway, Tanner saw the workmen and henchmen turn their fire away from him. Tanner now had his chance to reload his gun with bullets.

Still, Julius stood alone by the doorway. Remaining tempted to arm and throw his grenade into the warehouse. He watched on. Seeing Louis, his officers, the workmen, henchmen, Jade, and

Tyson fighting. Julius saw there would never be a better time to do some serious fatal damage to all his problems. Then, he could make up any explanation he would like to cover up his actions and what he was about to do.

On the walkway, Tanner's gun was fully reloaded.

Julius was ready to release the chain and throw the grenade into the warehouse. Tanner stood up on the walkway.

Julius looked up towards the ceiling of the warehouse towards the metal walkway. And there he saw Tanner.

Tanner looked down, seeing Julius in the doorway. Both their eyes met. Both stood still. Doing nothing, but wondering what the other was doing standing there.

Tanner was curious to know what Julius was planning.

Julius, seeing his former friend, knew Tanner would end up in the flame of the explosion. Standing on the walkway some fifty feet directly above where Jade was fighting Tyson, the temptation to throw the grenade in Jade's direction was so great.

Suddenly, the memories flooded Julius' mind. His past, long friendship with Tanner holding him back. He could not do it. Killing someone who was once his best friend. Even if it meant his chance to kill Jade would disappear, Julius' old friendship with Tanner was still holding him back.

Then Julius stepped back from the doorway. He lowered his arm, holding the grenade. The loose chain still attached. Sudden guilt came over Julius. He could not deal with it. Instead, he turned and walked away to leave the warehouse. Leaving Louis and his officers to fight by themselves.

Chapter 34

Jade and Tyson battled back and forth. Neither gave into their fight with the other.

Tyson continued hitting Jade hard with fists into her face and ribs. The parts of her body were already most wounded. Trying to make her fall and be defeated in the fight. But with every punch, Jade held her ground. Standing tall to take her shots at Tyson at any opportunity.

With every fist Jade shot at his face, Tyson stood stunned and surprised at Jade's resilience. He knew he had to give a lot more to take Jade down.

Tyson could hear the nearby gunfight between Kane's men and the police. He could see the men were now either wounded or dead.

He was running out of time.

Seeing Tyson was distracted, Jade took her chance. Fist after fist at Tyson's face. He was starting to look dazed and not hitting back.

Jade gave one last swing of a punch at Tyson. The impact making him stumble and lose balance.

Falling back several paces until he crashed into a nearby crate.

As he tried to wake up from his dazed state, he quickly spotted a crowbar nearby placed on top of a crate.

Now's my chance, Tyson thought.

Without hesitation, Tyson picked up the crowbar and began

storming back towards Jade.

Jade now saw the crowbar. She knew she was in trouble. She had no guns or weapons at hand.

Suddenly, she heard a loud gunshot nearby. She saw Tyson had stopped his approach and stood still.

Jade then spotted a circle of red blood had suddenly appeared on Tyson's shirt near the area of his shoulder. Now, the circle was starting to expand wider. Soaking more and more into his shirt.

Tyson knew what had just happened. He looked back at Jade. Getting weaker with every second. His wound making him lose strength in holding the crowbar. Then, it slipped out of his hand and fell to the ground. Making a loud clattering sound on impact. Instantly, Jade reached down for the crowbar and then threw it away. Making sure it was out of reach for Tyson to grab hold of it.

Taking a step back, Jade observed Tyson. Seeing him growing weak and in pain. His face colour turned purple. Then Tyson collapsed on the floor.

Jade now saw several feet away, standing behind Tyson, was Tanner. Standing at the bottom of the metal staircase. He lowered his gun that he had aimed at Tyson. What had seemed like a long time since they last saw each other, but had only been just a few hours, both Jade and Tanner took a moment at being relieved of seeing the other alive. For Jade, she knew she clearly had an ally and friend in Tanner.

Nearby, the gunfighting had stopped. Kane's men defeated, wounded, dead. Of those still alive, they had now surrendered.

Tanner walked up to Jade. With neither knowing what to say to the other, each raised a smile on their faces. Then Jade embraced Tanner. Holding him tight in her arms. For a moment,

Tanner felt surprised at Jade giving out this gesture. Then, he followed her lead and embraced her, too.

This was the first true embrace of a friendship that they had ever shown.

Nearby, Louis saw them both. He felt it proper to give them a moment alone. Then, seeing Tyson on the floor nearby, he approached his unconscious body. Lowering down, he grabbed hold of Tyson's hand to check his pulse. He had found it. Louis looked back at his officers giving his command.

'Get the medics out here! He's still alive!'

Now that they heard Louis, both Jade and Tanner let go of each other and stepped back a few paces.

Seeing them now apart, Louis stood up and walked towards Jade. He, too, was very relieved to see her alive.

'Thank God you're safe,' Louis said.

'I see you got my message,' replied Jade. 'Thanks for bringing the cavalry.'

'With what you showed in the photos and the chance of taking Kane in, I couldn't afford to lose the opportunity.'

'But there's one opportunity gone,' Tanner said. 'I saw a bunch of scientists escape. I think it might be best, Louis you give the order to track them down. Find out what they know.'

'I'll get to it,' Louis replied.

'What about Kane? Did you find him?' Jade asked.

'No. We thought he was in here with you,' Louis replied.

'He escaped too,' Jade said.

'Great. There went our chance. Now we'll never know where he's gone.'

Jade started searching her memory. Remembering all she heard Kane and Tyson say. 'The children,' Jade said quietly.

'What do you mean, Jade?' Tanner asked.

'I heard Tyson say something. Kane gave the order to kidnap the children. And he was keen to see them.'

'Did he say where they were?' Louis asked.

'Frank, all he said was that they'd be in the last place you wouldn't dare go to.'

With that comment, Tanner now knew where Kane had the children held hostage. With intent, Tanner started walking away. Both Jade and Louis watched him leave.

'Where's he going?' Louis asked. 'I'll find out,' Jade replied.

Jade then picked up her pace to walk alongside Tanner. 'Frank, where are you going?' Jade said.

'I know where the children are. We have to get there now,' Tanner said defiantly.

'And where's that?'

'I went and saw him when you were in jail. He must've been curious to know more about me and had a dossier set up about me and my past. I think he's gone there.'

'Gone where?'

'The place I used to call home.'

Chapter 35

It was still night time. Now, in the early hours of a cold morning. The city was cold, but in the countryside even colder.

Tanner drove his car with Jade as his passenger up towards the front of a derelict-looking large mansion. The headlights of his car lit up the driveway at the front of the house.

As Tanner switched off the car engine, he left the headlights on for a few more seconds. Giving him a chance to see for the first time in many years a place he once called home. Jade looked at the mansion. Feeling as if she recognised it, she could not place where she had seen it before.

'Get out your gun,' Tanner told Jade, which she did. Jade was relieved to have found it back in the warehouse before they left.

Then it dawned on her. She remembered where she knew this place from. The photo in Tanner's office.

'I've seen this house before. In the photo, you had back in your office. Who were the other two in the picture? Was that your wife and son?'

Tanner was hesitant to answer.

'Why did you move away from here? Why is no one living in it?' Jade knew there were more questions she was going to have to ask. And Tanner knew it.

'Jade, don't. Don't ask me. I don't want to remember what happened here.'

Then, Tanner opened his side car door. Wanting this

conversation to end. As a way to do this, he gave out the order to Jade.

'I'll check upstairs. You check the ground floor.'

Jade was hesitant to move. She wanted answers and wanted to know what Tanner was holding back.

'Jade, do as I say. He could kill those kids any minute.'

Suddenly, Jade sobered up her thoughts. Knowing the children's safety was the priority right now.

With that, Jade readied her gun. Opening her side door. Both left the car and started walking towards the front door of the large derelict mansion.

*

Opening the door, Jade and Tanner slowly made their way into the hallway. Up ahead to the left was the staircase. To the left and right were several closed doors to the ground floor rooms.

There was no carpet. Just wooden floorboards, dust, dirt, cobwebs, and silence. The house was very cold. Jade and Tanner's breathing misted up in the cold air. With the house so dark, Tanner tried to switch on the light. There was no electricity. Each took out torches from their coat pockets. Once switched on, they aimed their torches in the same direction as their guns.

Jade and Tanner gave each other one last gestured look. Then they split off and started searching the house. Tanner slowly walked towards the staircase. Taking each step up the stairs gently, trying not to make the floorboards creak underneath.

Jade made her way towards the back of the house. The kitchen and conservatory were placed there.

Reaching the kitchen door, she placed her gun on the closed

door and pushed it gently open. The kitchen area was empty. No one was there. At the far end were the windows looking out towards the large garden. Jade could start to see the first light of dawn beginning to break.

Turning away, Jade made her way back towards the front of the house.

Reaching the staircase, she noticed the door placed underneath the stairs. Possibly leading down to the cellar.

Again, she slowly opened the cellar door. Looking down, pointing her torch, she saw nothing of significance. But she knew that if she moved her torch away, the cellar would be pitch dark.

However, she could hear down below some faint sounds. The type of sounds she could not make out what they were.

Curious to know more, Jade slowly walked down the cellar staircase. Still pointing her torch and gun out in front.

Reaching the bottom, Jade quickly looked around her. Scanning as much of the cellar with her torch and eye as quickly as she could. It was even colder down in the cellar. The idea of being in a dark cellar for too long even made Jade start to become anxious and tense at what might be lurking out in the dark.

Then, in the distance, she heard more noise. Slowly, she walked forward to where she heard the sound coming from. Staying calm, Jade turned round a corner.

Then, what she saw gave her a small sense of relief and concern.

She had found the lost children.

Grouped together, they were all sat on the floor with their hands tied behind their backs, legs tied together in front and tape covering over their mouths. They were all seen to be tired, exhausted, dehydrated and had red eyes from having cried. Jade approached them carefully. Trying not to scare them. She lowered down, kneeled beside them, and started to undo their bonds. All the while trying to comfort them in their scared state.

'It's okay Don't be afraid. My name's Jade. I'm here to help you.'

But just then, Jade heard the cellar door slam shut from up above. She heard the turn of a key in the lock coming from the hallway.

It's Kane, Jade thought. *He's locked us down here.*

The children shouted out, scared. Jade tried to keep them calm. She knew she was now trapped.

And she knew Tanner was in trouble.

Chapter 36

On the first floor, Tanner carefully made his way across the landing. Already familiar with each room, he made his way towards the front of the house to what was the main bedroom.

Upon reaching the closed door, he stood still for a few seconds. Leaning his ear nearer the door, he could not hear anything inside. Complete silence.

Gently placing his hand on the door, he pushed it slowly open. Making the door creak and swing open.

Looking inside, the room was like the others. Bare, cold, and empty. The faint light of dawn was starting to light up the room. Letting Tanner see a rough outline of the room.

Standing still at the doorway, Tanner started having flashbacks to events earlier in his life that had taken place in this room. Some good, some bad and some just too painful.

Distracted by his thoughts, Tanner paid no attention to the presence walking along the landing up behind him. The presence of Kane, holding a metal pipe in his hand. Moving forward towards his target.

Kane struck the pipe on the back of Tanner's head. Making Tanner fall forward to the ground in the main bedroom. The strike of the pipe shocked Tanner that he lost grip of his gun that was now on the floor right by where Kane now stood over him.

Tanner looked up, dazed at the sight of Kane standing in the doorway. Kane spotted the fallen gun and lowered down to pick it up. Standing up straight, he now pointed the gun down at

Tanner.

Tanner made himself wake up from the blow. Looking up at Kane, his thoughts and feelings turned to anger. All from having the memory and pain he associated with this room beginning to surface once again.

'You had to choose here to hide away, didn't you?' Tanner said.

'After our talk at the restaurant, I had Tyson do a full check on your past,' Kane said. 'So, this is where it happened? Am I, right? This room. Where the deed was done, she was standing where I am right now. Yes?'

'Shut up. Just shut up,' Tanner said angrily.

'No. No. The Sins of Frank Tanner. They're not just ghosts that stay within these four walls. You carry them with you every single day of your life.'

'I deserved what I got.'

'Spoken like a guilty man. A truly guilty man.'

Kane lowered himself down, still pointing the gun at Tanner. Kane wanted to take a closer look at Tanner's face.

'But you know what, Frank? You look a lot like your father. He was a long-time enemy of my mentor. We both aspire to be like our mentors. Your father was yours. He had all the qualities and strengths you wished to have as well. You just weren't strong enough to follow his example of how to be a man, a husband and a father.'

'You can't know the whole story, Kane,' replied Tanner.

'But I do.' Kane rose to his feet. 'I know everything about you. You've lost a lot in your life. You lost the future mapped out for you. The life that could've been. And it all started right here in this very room.'

'Are the children here that you hid away?'

'Yes. In the last place I thought you'd never dare go back to. The dark black hole of your past in this house. So, how does it feel? Being back in this room. The room where your wife found you screwing another woman on the very bed you shared together?'

Kane had now touched the deepest nerve within Tanner. The most sensitive, painful part of his heart had just had a knife stab right through it with those words.

'There's no more pain you can give me than what's already there. No more than what I carry around with me every single day,' Tanner said.

'Really? Maybe it's time I gave it a try.'

Kane readied to shoot Tanner in the heart. Tanner knew he was living the last seconds of his life.

He knew Kane would pull the trigger. And he knew he was going to die in the place he once called home.

BANG!

The trigger was pulled. The bullet hit its target. The wound made him go into shock. His chest began to bleed.

And the gun dropped out of the wounded Kane's hand.

Kane collapsed on the floor from the gunshot. Striking him in his back.

Jade stood on the landing. Aiming her gun where Kane once stood. Having escaped the cellar by ramming open the locked door, she had quietly made her way up the staircase once she heard voices coming from the floor above. Hearing the voices from a distance, it was difficult for her to make out what was being said. But on seeing him, she could make out the silhouette, posture, and voice of Jack Kane. Aiming her gun at him, she felt relief to see him fall to the floor.

Once fallen, Jade walked across the landing towards the

doorway of the main bedroom. Not taking her eyes off Kane's body, she looked down on him with disdain. Then, standing above him, she spoke with a quiet, passionate confidence.

'Don't ever mess with an angry bitch. Prick.'

With that, Jade lowered her gun. Relieved, Tanner started to pick himself up off the floor.

'I'm so glad to see you,' Tanner said. 'Now that we've both saved the other person tonight, are we even?'

'You could say that,' replied Jade. 'I found the children. They're downstairs in the basement.'

'Good. I've got to get out of this room.'

Jade noticed how uncomfortable Tanner suddenly became. Seeing him quickly stand up, leave the room, and move quickly away from Jade, she had never seen him act this way before.

'Is there anything you want to tell me?' Jade asked him. Tanner stopped walking along the landing and looked back at Jade.

'Like what?'

'You don't seem yourself.'

'I'm fine, Jade. Don't worry. We got Kane. And the kids are safe. That's good enough for now.'

Tanner smiled at Jade to reassure her. Jade smiled back at Tanner to reassure him, but inside, she remained unconvinced. But she did not show it.

What were you both talking about? Jade thought.

She knew something was wrong, but she felt it best to let it rest for today. If Tanner had nothing left to share, there was nothing more to talk about.

'I'll go take care of the children. I'll phone Louis and tell him where we are,' Tanner said as he walked down the staircase, making his way to the cellar.

Jade watched him go. Seeing him get out his mobile phone and making the call to Louis. *Back to the old Tanner,* Jade thought. *Trying to keep himself busy.*

Now, with Tanner out of sight, Jade turned her attention back to Kane.

Outside the bedroom windows, the dawn had finally come. But grey clouds in the distance were moving in.

Jade could hear something from beneath her. Kane was lying there unconscious from his wound. But as she lowered down, she could hear the faint sound of Kane breathing. He was still alive.

With that knowledge, Jade had a wry smile rise up on her face. Jade thought, *What shall I do with you now?*

Chapter 37

Kane woke up. He could see nothing. Pitch black. But he was moving side to side, out of control. He could hear the faint sound of an engine. The sound of fast screeching tyres.

Kane quickly realised he was in the boot of a car.

Suddenly, the car screeched to a halt. The momentum made Kane bang his head on the hood of the car. The pain from his wound made him shout out in agony. The car had stopped moving. The engine was kept running. Kane could start to hear the trickle of rain hitting the car boot outside.

Then Kane heard footsteps walking to the back of the car.

Suddenly, the car boot opened. The daylight from outside was hurting Kane's eyes. The rain hitting Kane's face was now making him well and truly wake up.

And then he saw her. Jade. Standing above him. From his point of view, he saw the grey clouds being directly behind Jade's face. The rain dripped down her hair and face. Her face again wet and her long black hair soaked. Kane was in trouble. And he knew it. Big time.

'Nice car you have here, Kane' Jade said. 'I found it parked nearby the mansion. Such a clean pretty car. But your bloody wound is going to mess up such a clean car boot.'

With that comment, Jade picked up Kane. Tossing him out, she threw him hard down on the wet floor. The pain from his wound made Kane scream out.

He looked around him to see where he was. Jade had driven

Kane down to the old city docks.

Jade placed the car on one of the piers. Now, with a gun in hand, Jade had been waiting for this moment.

On the ground, Kane looked up towards Jade. Slowly, Jade started moving to stand directly above Kane. Kane began to panic.

'Jade listen to me. You don't want to do this.'

'That's what you really think?'

'Just turn me in to the police. That's your job, isn't it? Do your job.'

'I could do that. Maybe l should. But not today.'

Kane's heart began to race quicker. He started crawling his body along the small pier. Crawling further away from Jade. She allowed him to and was in no rush to stop him from such a futile gesture. He was soon reaching the end of the pier. And Jade casually walked forward to stand above the wounded Kane once again.

'Any last words, Kane?'

'Jade, I'm tired. I'm fading here. Please. Turn me in.'

'After all that you've done to me?' Jade shouted out angrily. 'You've made me suffer my whole life. You killed my parents when I was a baby. You got two of your gang to kill my son. Have I not suffered enough for you?'

Kane looked up, puzzled at Jade. 'What do you mean?'

'You hired the two men that blew up my son.'

Suddenly, Kane smiled and started to chuckle and laugh.

'What's so funny?' Jade said.

'Well, you do get around making enemies, Jade.'

'What?' Jade said confused.

'It wasn't me,' Kane said. 'I didn't hire them to kill your son. Someone else did. Someone else who wants to

207

see you suffer.'

With that revelation, Kane continued to laugh. Jade was now full of anger. She had been wrong about Kane giving the order to kill her son. But still, she was looking down on the man who killed her parents.

Kane was laughing. Finding the whole thing to be a big joke.

But when Jade lifted up her gun, pointing it at his head, he was not laughing any more. Jade stared right into his eyes. Kane looked right back into hers.

'Go on. Do it,' Kane said. 'I know you want to kill me.' Jade said nothing for a few seconds.

Then she spoke calmly, 'That's where you're wrong, Kane.'

At that moment, Jade moved the aim of her gun. Shooting Kane in his left leg. Making him scream out in pain.

Then she aimed her gun at his right leg. Shooting him again. He continued to scream.

And again, moving her aim and, in quick succession, shooting his left and right arms. The screams of Kane continued to echo out loud into the air.

Then Jade lowered her gun. Looking down at Kane. The pain and agony of the wounds showed all over his face.

'I didn't want to be the one to kill you, Kane. That wasn't at the front of my mind. I just wanted the chance to see you suffer.'

Kane looked up at Jade. Not knowing what was coming next. Then Jade spoke, 'And also knowing I was the last person you ever saw.'

With that, Jade kicked Kane hard in the stomach. Pushing him off the edge of the pier. Making him fall into the water below.

Kane was struggling to stay afloat. The wounds from his chest, arms and legs were too painful for him to move. Looking up, Jade stood motionless. Letting Kane slowly die.

Panic started to set in for Kane. His mouth, eyes and head were starting to fall under the water. He could not swim from all the pain. He could not hold himself up for much longer. He screamed out in fear one last time.

'JADE!'

But Jade did nothing. Looking down, Kane's head went underwater. Slowly, the waters began to calm down from the panic splashing.

No sign of Kane's body above water.

Then, the bubbles from beneath the surface slowly stopped bubbling up. Slowly. Slowly. Then. Nothing. Silence. Calm. Peace.

Jade stood all alone on the pier. The rain continued to fall. Jade had finally got revenge and justice for her parents.

Chapter 38

'The reign of Jack Kane is over,' Mayor Gordon said.

He was standing by a podium on a stage in the main hall of Alpha City's Town Hall.

Speaking to a crowd of news reporters, cameramen, photographers, and the general public. All of whom had been invited to attend this special ceremony.

Commemorating the successful work done by Jade and Tanner. Both of which stood on the stage behind Mayor Gordon.

In attendance sat in the front row were Julius Carver and Louis Walker. Louis was looking happy and pleased for both of his friends. Julius looked more reserved. Having no smile on his face, he still remained polite in his demeanour for the sake of this public appearance.

Both Julius, Louis, Tanner, Jade, and everyone else in attendance continued to listen to the mayor's big speech.

'This city is united as one once again. All of Kane's associates have been arrested and placed in jail. All this would not have been possible without the efforts of the Alpha City Police Department. And also, by the efforts of two very special people. This city owes a great debt to these two private detectives. Their passion, drive and goals aim to bring justice to those most in need. We hereby congratulate them both for their efforts and their success. By finding the major criminals that have plagued our city in recent times, we say thank you. Please step forward. Private Detective Frank Tanner. Private Detective Jade

Hall.'

With that, Jade, and Tanner both stepped forward towards Mayor Gordon. Gordon hands them both an honorary medal.

'Congratulations, both of you,' Mayor Gordon said privately to both of them.

The audience started to applaud and all stood up to give a huge ovation to the both of them.

The photographers flashed their cameras at them. They both smiled. The television cameras zoomed in close on them.

Jade appreciated the gesture that had been given to her. She looked out into the crowd. Seeing Louis smiling and clapping. Looking at the far end of the hall, she recognised someone else.

It was Luke. Clapping, applauding, and smiling. He stood there looking on proudly at Jade. This was his way of saying thank you for what you did. By being at the ceremony, this was Luke's way of saying you deserve this moment. And that she should be proud of what she has achieved in her life.

Nearby, Julius looked up at the two of them on the stage. He stopped clapping. He pondered briefly. Feeling grateful Jade did kill Kane. And by doing so, she had wiped away the threat of blackmail Kane had hanging over Julius in regards to their past dealings. He could now relax knowing he was safe and in the clear.

Suddenly, in his pocket, he felt the vibration from his mobile phone. Someone had sent him a text.

Taking his phone out, the message read: 'BE PATIENT AND LOYAL TO ME.'

With that, Julius knew there was still more to come in the future for Tanner and Jade. But for now, he would let them have their moment as heroes.

Up on the stage, Jade and Tanner turned and looked at each

other. Tanner leaned over to speak a quiet word to Jade.

'Your parents and Sean would be very proud of you, Jade.'

With that comment, Jade continued to smile. But there was now a thought on her mind. A thought she could not shake away.

She thought, I needed to see my son.

Chapter 39

Later that day, Jade had made her way to Southern Cemetery. Walking around the graves of children passed on.

Holding a bunch of flowers, she reached the gravestone of her son Sean. On the gravestone was a photo of Sean smiling.

Jade gently lowered down to place the flowers by his gravestone. Standing up, she stood quietly, looking at the photo.

Nearby, she heard the footsteps of someone approaching. She did not turn to see who it was. But she already had an idea of who it might be.

It was Tanner. He stood side by side with Jade. Himself also looking at the photo of Sean on the gravestone.

'I thought you'd come here,' Tanner said quietly.

'I needed to,' Jade replied. 'I never got the chance to before. They didn't let me go to his funeral.'

'I know. I was here. I felt like it was the right thing to do for you and Sean.'

'I could've done more.'

'You did all you could, Jade. You got justice for him. You got Kane. He ordered him to be killed.'

'No. Kane killed my parents. I got them justice. But he wasn't the one who ordered Sean to be killed.'

'What do you mean?'

'Those two men who put the explosion together were hired by someone else'

'Who?'

'I don't know. But one day, whoever hired them, they'll let me know. Until that day, it's not over.'

Jade walked a few paces forward towards the gravestone. Placing her hand on her lips, she gently kissed her fingers. Then she placed the kissed fingers on Sean's photo.

'Sweet dreams, my angel,' Jade said. 'I hope your grandparents keep you safe and loved.'

Jade then started to walk away from the cemetery alone. Tanner stayed behind. Letting Jade leave the cemetery by herself.

Tanner looked on in pride at the person who walked away. The journey Jade had taken was one she was still taking. A journey that would keep her fighting on, to live each day as it comes. Live to make her parents and son proud of her every single day of her life.

What a journey you've been on in your life, Jade, Tanner thought.

And her journey was far from over.

Chapter 40

Night time had fallen once again over Alpha City. The lights of the city were a sight to behold.

Louis stood alone on the rooftop of Alpha Central Police Station. Looking out over the city, the night sky was clear and calm.

'Beautiful view.'

Louis turned around. He recognised the voice.

It was Jade. Wearing her long black coat, white shirt, black jeans, and black high heeled leather boots. Her long straight black hair was caught in the wind making it gently move in the breeze. Jade looked refreshed and energised.

After what Jade had just said, Louis thought for that moment that she was wrong, it was she herself that looked a beautiful sight. But he could dare not let her know that. He was still on duty and this was an official appointment.

'Yes. You're right. It's a very lovely night,' Louis said hiding what he felt was the truth.

'I got your message.' Jade started walking towards Louis. 'You wanted to see me about something?'

'Well, first of all I wanted to say well done. For the job you did. *A* lot of people in the Police Force thought it wasn't possible to see the fall of Kane. But you did it, Jade. You've changed things for this city. For the better.'

'Only for now Louis. You never know what's around the corner. You'll always find a new fight that needs fighting.'

'True. And sometimes we can be given a sign of what we'll find round the corner.'

'What do you mean?' Jade asked.

'Well, back at the main Alpha City Police Headquarters, we had an envelope delivered to us earlier tonight. This is why I wanted to see you.'

'Why?'

Louis took out the envelope from his coat pocket. He handed it over to Jade. 'Because the envelope was addressed to you,' Louis said.

Jade, now curious, took the envelope and started tearing it open. Inside, she took out a small letter.

It read:

JADE. I'M COMING OUT OF THE SHADOWS TO FIND YOU, HEAR MY BIG BANG SOON.

LOVE

CARA HELLER

LEADER OF TEKKER

x

Placed on top of the name, Cara Heller, was the mark of a lipstick kiss. Jade's curiosity and interest had risen. She was hooked wanting to know more.

'She wants to meet me,' Jade said.

'Who?'

'Cara Heller. Leader of the group known as Tekker.'

'Do you know her?' Louis asked.

'No. I've heard the name of the group several times. She's got me interested. I'll need to be ready for her. Until then, I'll be waiting.'

Feeling the conversation was over, Jade began to walk away from Louis. But Louis had one last question for Jade.

'So, are you ready to get back to work?'

Jade stopped, looked around at Louis and gave her answer. 'I never stopped Louis. And I never will.'

Jade had nothing more to say. She turned back and continued to walk away. Leaving Louis alone on the rooftop. Louis looked on in admiration at Jade. Smiling, knowing Jade was truly back in the game.

Chapter 41

The next day, Jade was back at 68 Dale Street, back at the Private Detective offices. Walking up to her office door, she stood back to look at the name printed on it.

PRIVATE DETECTIVE JADE HALL.

A sense of pride came over her. Then a smile rose up on her face. She was back where she needed to be.

Then, placing her hand on the door handle, she opened the door to her office. Ready for the day ahead. Ready for work. Ready to do what she does best.

Epilogue

Many hundreds of miles away, a female figure stood watching the television screen. She was watching the ceremony of Mayor Gordon giving honorary medals to both Jade and Tanner in Alpha City.

The female was currently taking a break from an important session. She looked and stared at Jade on the screen. Feeling like a predator ready to hunt her next prey.

But first things first. Her session was not over.

Leaving the room the television was in, the female walked down a long landing towards an open bedroom door.

Wearing a tight black leather catsuit, black tights, black leather boots and long latex black gloves, she held onto her long leather black whip as she reached the open bedroom doorway.

Speaking into the bedroom, a young man had his hands and feet each tied to the four corner bed posts. Spread naked across the bed.

'Leo,' the female said. 'Mistress Cara has an appointment to make in Alpha City. But first, it's time I gave you your reward.'

At that moment, the female entered the bedroom. Looking down at her submissive, she slammed the door shut.

Cara Heller's night had only just begun.

THE END.